Quilted Quick and Dead

An Anna Rendle, Joe Brown Mystery

by Barbara E. Moss

DORRANCE
PUBLISHING CO
EST. 1920
PITTSBURGH, PENNSYLVANIA 15238

Dorrance Publishing Co
585 Alpha Drive
Suite 103
Pittsburgh, PA 15238
Visit our website at *www.dorrancebookstore.com*

ISBN: 978-1-4809-9486-7

eISBN: 978-1-4809-9443-0

Chapter One

"Hello! Aunt Sarah!" I peered through the screen door. The big, oak front door stood ajar. An autumn breeze sifted in over my shoulder and rhythmically flicked the front pages of the *New Bedford Standard Times* lying folded in half on the telephone stand in the front hall. The pages made a gentle slapping sound, the only sound emanating from my aunt's hallway. Receiving no answer after calling several more times, I went inside and called my aunt again. Odd. Where was she? She must be home because the door was unlocked. But it was odd she left the heavy door standing open.

I kept calling her name as I walked through the first-floor rooms: the very Victorian formal parlor, the sitting room, dining room, bath, kitchen, and even the little greenhouse room she had off her kitchen where she spent hours tending her prized African violets. I found no sign of her.

I went upstairs. My aunt's house had four rooms and a large bathroom on the second floor. All the doors were shut but for her bedroom door which stood wide open, the sunshine streaming through and making a yellow pool of light on the hall floor.

There she was! Lying in bed. Her favorite quilt, the one with brick red and dark green interlocking circles and stars against a cream background, covered her to her armpits. Her thin arms lay neatly at her sides above the quilt. Later, something about that quilt would seem wrong to me. But now, surprised to find my aunt in bed in the middle of the afternoon, I didn't try to pinpoint what it was.

I stepped just inside the doorway of her room. "Aunt Sarah?" I whispered softly. Now I could see her eyes were wide open, very wide open. Her hands lay palms up. But her pillow was on the floor, propped unnaturally against the box spring, giving the lie to a scene of peaceful repose.

"Aunt Sarah?" I called louder and walked up to the bed. "Aunt Sarah!" I shrieked. Her face was so distorted with bulging eyes. "Aunt Sarah!" I grabbed her shoulders as if to shake her awake. She felt cool. I had lifted her but slightly, when a stench began to drift through the room. Excrement. My dear and very proper aunt had messed herself.

I ran back down the stairs to the front hall where her telephone was. She had always been adamant nothing would happen necessitating a bedside phone. Hurriedly grabbing the receiver, I dialed 191, no, 119, no, then 911. "Please, I want an ambulance, a doctor, no, the police! I don't know what to say. It's my aunt!" I gave the address.

"Please, stay on the line," the calming voice responded. But I slammed down the receiver as my stomach heaved and my mouth filled. I ran to the downstairs bathroom.

When the ambulance arrived, all blinking and flashing lights, followed by a police car, I was watching for them at the front door, shakily peeping through the lacy curtain that covered the door's oval glass.

Two uniformed policemen and two EMTs came to the door. Some other men stood on the sidewalk.

"Ma'am, we had a call."

"Yes, yes," I cried. "My aunt is very ill. She's

upstairs." I motioned to the mahogany staircase that filled half the front hall.

Three men tramped up the stairs. One uniformed officer insisted I stay below "just to give them room to work" as he put it. He stayed with me until a call of: "Hey, Joe! Take a look." brought him up to my aunt's room.

Long moments passed. I heard voices upstairs, perhaps phone calls. More cars pulled up to the house. And more men entered. Two stopped to speak to me.

"I am Detective Pereira, Per Pereira, and this is Dr. Medeiros, the medical examiner," said a gaunt sandy-haired man of the stubby man beside him. The doctor sported a thick black mustache and was as swarthy as the detective was fair. They went upstairs. I was asked again to stay below, and the police officer named Joe came back down as if to keep an eye on me.

A cold tingling knotted my scalp and an icy chill ran down my neck, spreading across my shoulders and down my back. My insides rolled. I felt my heart slamming against my ribs. I kept thinking, *"Medical examiner? Why don't they take her to the hospital?"*

Maybe a hot cup of tea would settle down the tumult in my stomach. Both my mother and Aunt Sarah always said a hot cup of tea made life's problems more manageable. We were all big tea drinkers. I went down the hall to the kitchen at the back of the house and dragged the kettle across the stove to the front burner.

I listened to the sounds from upstairs, hoping to hear my aunt's voice as the EMTs brought her around; the uniformed man hung in the hallway just outside the kitchen door. Annoyed they had separated me from my aunt, I turned my back to him.

Before the water boiled, more vehicles pulled up to the house. I stepped out again into the hall as several men clambered up the staircase with assorted gear. I recognized only a camera among the paraphernalia.

Then the kettle whistled, and I poured the boiling water over a teabag. I wrapped my hands around the hot mug feeling its healing warmth sink into my palms and a little of the tightness between my shoulder blades softened. I sat down at the table and, slumping over this small comfort, wept.

Some moments later, worn of weeping, I lifted my face and wiped my tears with my palms. A white square—a handkerchief—dangled before my bleary eyes. Det. Pereira sat at the end of the table offering his handkerchief.

"Will you be all right, miss?"

"Yes, I'm okay. It's Mrs., Mrs. Rendle. Anna Rendle."

"The de-er—the woman upstairs was known to you?"

"She is my aunt. Sarah Spears. Can't all those men do anything?"

"Mrs. Rendle, there is no good way to put this. I'm afraid your aunt has passed on."

"She is dead? Oh, dear Lord!"

"Yes, I'm afraid so, Mrs. Rendle. Did she live alone?"

"Yes."

At this point, I heard sounds from the hall and ran out into the hallway. Mr. Pereira followed me, close behind, but did not try to stop me.

Through the rails, I saw a man's legs coming down the stairs backwards. His hands steadied a stretcher-like contraption, its two wheels bumping and shaking its small package as it bounced to each step. A second man steered from the upper end. When the contraption reached the hall, a second pair of wheels sprung down like landing gear on a plane, and the little canvas-bagged form of my aunt on the wheeled gurney was rolled across the hall and out onto the porch. I wrapped my arms around my stomach squeezing to steady my rolling insides and stiffen my spine. I turned away. She, her body, seemed so tiny now, I thought.

With no ado whatsoever, permitting no reflection on my part, the detective immediately said, "There are a few questions I must ask you, Mrs. Rendle."

"Why?"

"Is there someplace where we can sit down?"

I ushered him into the room on the left at the base of the stairs. The room across the hall to the right of the front door was a formal parlor and not used much, but this room across from it was her real sitting room.

Aunt Sarah's living room had a ruby oriental rug on the floor and heavy velvet drapes that picked up the same deep red tone. Long-tailed pale golden birds subtly patterned the ivory wallpaper. Their curving plumage gave a quiet paisley effect to the paper. Aunt Sarah had replaced the Victorian furniture with two comfortable easy chairs and a couch, making the room cozy and inviting.

I offered him a chair and sat in the one by the piano. I loved this room. I had spent many a happy afternoon and evening with my aunt in this room, laughing with her friends and singing as she played. On this afternoon, the room seemed to beg for my aunt's laughter. Another chill and a prickly sensation ran down my neck and back. Something was wrong with the room or with its furnishings. I couldn't place it, but something was very wrong.

"Now, she was you aunt?"

"Yes, my Aunt Sarah Spears, wife of my father's brother."

"How old?"

"Seventy-five, but in very fine health." I dabbed at my eyes with the handkerchief. "I suppose it's a blessing she went so peacefully."

"Er, ahem," was all Mr. Pereira said, shifting in his chair and crossing and uncrossing his legs as I worked the hankie around my eyes and blew my nose.

"Mrs. Rendle, why did you come to see your aunt today? Do you come often, by invitation, or...?"

I explained how like a surrogate mother she was— so sweet, accepting, and supportive. How she helped with my brother's and sister's children and never seemed to mind or even realize how much of herself she was giving. "She was so sweet, so dear. Everyone loved her."

"They're all like that," he muttered to himself.

"Who are?" I looked up sensing something in his voice not there before.

"Loved by everyone, not an enemy in the world, the 'Aunt Sarah's'."

A protesting lump rose in my throat. I thought he was being a little sarcastic. How could anyone imply anything negative about my aunt?

"But she *was* good. Gave to every charity that asked, couldn't pass a bum on the street without putting something in his hand."

"Mrs. Rendle, why did you come here today?"

"She had asked me to stop by sometime to see her new violets," I said and added quickly, "She raised African violets, you see. And thought she had developed a new strain—a double two-toned peach and orange one. She was very proud of it. Thought she might raise and sell it commercially. She was trying to come up with a suitable name for the variety."

"Did you like it?"

"I never saw it."

"Why not?

"Oh, my God, my God!"

"Okay. It's okay, Mrs. Rendle. This is a bad time." He began to lever his long body out of the chair.

"I came up to the house—the door was open—unusual—I called—no answer—I came into the house called and called, walked all around downstairs, and then went upstairs and I...I... Oh, God!"

"Mrs. Rendle, Officer Roderiques will take you home, but I must tell you there will be an autopsy, and I will need to speak to you again."

I wiped around my eyes and nose again, still using his handkerchief. He took my elbow and turned me over to Officer Roderiques.

I dabbed my eyes and wiped at my nose all the way to my house, which was really just a long walk from my aunt's home. As we approached my house, a large green car eased away from the curb by my drive and then picked up speed as the police cruiser approached.

"Humph, Lincoln Town Car. Friends of yours?" asked the, until then, silent Roderiques.

"No, no way. Maybe they were collecting for something or trying to save my soul. You know, Jehovah Witnesses or something."

"Pretty tough looking brutes for religious types," said the officer catching a glimpse of the two men as their car sped by.

Chapter Two

The next morning bright yellow sunshine streamed into the bedroom. Oomph! Rollo, my middle-aged cat, jumped up on my chest and began a kneading dance, pounding his feet into my breasts. Painful. I lifted my head from the pillow and saw my cat tossing his head joyously. Yuck! He had a huge mouse clenched between his jaws and was flipping it like a dish-rag up and down in time with his dance.

"Rollo, get out of here." I threw back the covers. My feet hit the floor just as Rollo scurried under the bed still clutching his juicy prey.

"Sorry, honey. I saw him from the corner of my eye. He slipped through the cat flap all sneaky-like. I should have known." Steve, my husband, was apologizing from the doorway. Then he dropped to his knees and peered under the bed.

"Get out of here, Rollo. Here, give me that mouse."

Our family cat had such a strong Yankee work ethic he brought home the "bacon" almost every morning. Rollo was white and black like a Holstein cow, but without any bovine placidity whatsoever.

"He was up here earlier, but you were zonked," Steve added, still on his knees.

"What time is it?"

"9:30."

I shuffled into the bathroom, giving my hair a primitive combing with my fingers. I came downstairs some minutes later wrapped in my old fuzzy bathrobe and grabbed a steaming mug of coffee. Rollo was washing his ear with vigor proportionate to his pique.

"Did you get the mouse?"

"In the garbage can. Only a few scratches."

Steve held up his hands to display his battle wounds, a few scratches around his wrists. I dropped into my chair and he slid half a grapefruit before me and sat down across the table. Gently, he reached for my hand. I could tell by the way he was leaning toward me he had something more to say.

"Steve, please don't say anything about Aunt Sarah. At least not until I've had some toast and coffee," I said, pushing his hand aside.

"Ann, I must speak with you. Aunt Sarah did not die of natural causes. The police were here shortly before you got up. She was murdered."

"No! How can that be?"

"Apparently, it was obvious to them yesterday when they found the body. She had been smothered. Naturally, the detective didn't want to upset you more than you already were. Now, honey, crying's not going to help."

"Oh, goodness, goodness." I broke into tears and started shaking all over. It was all back again–her face, the bedroom, the teakettle, the quilt. The quilt? There was something about that quilt.

Later in the morning, the front doorbell rang with its abrupt "buh-rinnng". It was an old-fashioned bell that rang by the twist of a knob. The kids on the block loved it. Today I would have welcomed a school kid taking a dare and listened for the clump of a boy's feet running down our front steps. But it was Wednesday morning and the neighborhood kids were all in school.

Steve received Detective Pereira and Officer Roderiques. I ran upstairs where I dabbed on some makeup to cover the tear stains, blew my nose, and combed my hair. I smoothed my turtleneck over my jeans and after a few moments strode into our living room feigning a calmness I certainly didn't feel. Cops were in my house demanding to talk to me. Dear God! Steve leaned against the doorway to the dining room. Officer Roderiques had already taken a seat on the little Queen Anne chair by our secretary desk. Pulling a bath towel off the end couch cushion, I offered the detective a seat, remarking guests got the cat hair-free seat and the rest of us went around as fuzzy pseudo-cats. No response to my attempt at humor. A quiet minute passed. I felt embarrassed by my attempt at levity and then downright nervous under his fixed gaze.

"Are you the next of kin?"

"No, she has a son and, I believe, a daughter from her first marriage."

The detective pulled out a notebook from his suit coat pocket and carefully unscrewed a beautiful black pen, placing the notebook on his knee, he raised a questioning eyebrow at me.

"Her son is Captain Matthias Spears and her daughter she referred to as 'Cookie'—I don't know her real name or her last name or where she lives, but I think she is in Illinois."

"Her son?"

"He is a widower, lost his wife to cancer five years ago. Has two sons in college in Maine. Him, you can't reach."

"Try me."

I felt a little surge of smugness. "He is on a nuclear submarine. Only God and Uncle Sam know where he is."

"All right then, Mrs. Rendle, someone will have to identify the body and you seem..."

"Oh, my." The tears were brimming again, and I reached over and pulled a tissue from the box on the lamp stand.

While I was trying to collect myself, he hastily interjected, "Well, a friend then. Who are her friends?"

"Well, she did a lot with the ladies in the sewing circle at St. Paul's, Marta Jensen, Priscilla Bronstad, and Solveig Gundersen." I wondered fleetingly if his first name was Norwegian and if he had any ties to the folks at St. Paul's. Uncle Matthias was a Quaker, but Aunt

Sarah, being from the Midwest, had always kept her Lutheran identity and spent every Wednesday with the sewing group.

I gave him their addresses. I gave the names of others she knew and the names of her doctor and lawyer. Then I remembered the African violet club. Letitia Marston was head of it and came to see my aunt often. Letitia would know her friends in that organization, I told him. "Letitia knows everything."

"Any men in her life?"

"She was seventy-five!" He waited. "Well, there was old Joe. You know how charitable I told you Aunt Sarah was. She was always helping people. She once remarked, kind of offhand like, that poor Joe had such a hard time or such a hard life or something like that."

"His name?"

"Something ordinary. Ah—Brown! Yes! Joe Brown."

"Address?"

"No idea."

"How did your aunt 'help' him?"

"Well, I don't know exactly. She didn't talk about him much. Once I came over when she was cooking something for him."

"Oh? And did he live with her?"

"No! I mean, not like that! I mean maybe he rented a room from her for a while, but I don't really know. Certainly, there wasn't anything, uh, you know. He kept some things there," I volunteered and then regretted my words. "Never volunteer," my army-vet father had told me once. I could see in my mind's eye my dad's pink face, shiny bald head, and the twinkle in his eye as he shook a finger at me.

"What things?"

I told him how Aunt Sarah would say things like: "Oh, that toolbox belongs to Joe." He'd left a cardboard box on the floor of the back porch and maybe a suitcase; I was not sure what all was there. But I thought I could identify them.

"Description? Of this Joe Brown?"

"Late sixties, broad shoulders, gruff. Actually, I only really met him once or so."

"How'd you meet him?"

"Aunt Sarah introduced us when I came over one day, and he was leaving. She said he was an old friend of her husband, relocating, as she called it."

"Think," Pereira said softly, "what else did he say as he left? When was this that you met him?"

"It was a year ago last fall. I remember exactly because I had come with my postcards to show her."

"Were these old postcards? Collectibles? Why were you bringing postcards?"

"No, new. They were hot off the press. I drew the pictures. I had just picked them up. I want to be an artist."

Steve sort of snickered and mumbled, "About as small time as one can get."

Pereira turned toward him and frowned, then nodded for me to go on. "Tell me."

I took a deep breath and tried to explain concisely. But a forty-two-year history took some sorting out. I explained how I grew up in Acushnet and always liked to draw and drew on everything, even the walls, when I was a kid. My mom worked long, hot hours in a laundry and dry-cleaners, and Dad was a mechanic. They made a decent living, but it wasn't easy raising four kids. My brothers and sister all went to New Bedford Voke. They got good vocational training and real jobs. But I was the weird one. I dreamed of going to art school, saved my babysitting money, and after high school started at Paine School of Art. I had some scholarship money, lived at home, and worked an evening shift at Cumberland Farms where they would only let me work until 7:00 P.M. because of possible robbers. I worked every evening 4 to 7. Even so, I needed loans to finish. I got an art-related job, at least, it was art in my parents' opinion. I worked silk screening T-shirts for a gift shop in the historic district. Moby Dick's great tail rising from the sea and thrashing whaleboats in five versions and three colors. Tedious, but it paid the bills.

Then I met Steve at an exhibit. He had a doctorate in American Literature and was teaching at the community college. He got me interested in teaching. We married. I took education courses and began teaching art in the elementary schools.

"The postcards?" The detective cross and uncrossed his legs, obviously impatient.

"Well, I'm just getting to that," I responded.

I summarized quickly, saying I taught ten years then had an accident. My cousin had a motorcycle and took me for a ride. He gave me his helmet. It was still hard to talk about. He was in a wheelchair. I broke some ribs and hurt my back. I couldn't stand for a long time, so I had to stop teaching and went back to painting and drawing. One of my little successes was a set of historic New Bedford scenes—pen and ink sort of things—I had made into postcards and sold them locally in a gift shop. They were selling quite nicely now.

I couldn't help but add, although my income from

them was just a few dollars a month. "But that day, my first batch was just off the press and I was so proud of them. I wanted my aunt to see them."

Detective Pereira shifted in his seat. "Does this bring us to Joe Brown?"

"He was standing in her doorway when I arrived deep in conversation with my aunt." I almost went on my way, I told the detective, because my aunt looked so intent and he stood there gently swinging a suitcase so big I didn't think I could have lifted it. "He is a big, brawny ape of a man."

"A seaman?"

"No, I don't think so. For all his brawn, his skin was very pale and smooth. How I remember him at all was because I heard him call my aunt 'Sari'. Only Uncle Matthias had called her that. Once they saw me, she introduced me, saying he was a friend of Matthias', and he left quickly."

"Did she tell you anything, ever, about him?"

"Only that time when I asked who he was. She said, with kind of a mysterious twinkle in her eye, he was 'a voice from the past.' Then we talked about the postcards. I heard his name mentioned maybe only one more time."

"When?" came the laconic question.

"Couldn't tell you. And I don't think I know for sure who mentioned him to me. One of the women, Priscilla Bronstad, or maybe Letitia."

At the thought of the very fluffy, feminine Letitia, I looked down at my ink-stained nails and realized I hadn't been using the tissue. My eyes were dry. I was so wrapped up in recounting my own biography. Did indulging the ego strengthen the spirit? I wondered fleetingly.

"Detective Pereira, I will go to identify my aunt's body. In fact, sir, I would rather go than pass off the duty to one of her friends." I could imagine the wonderful chatter there'd be, in English and Norwegian, at the sewing circle if one of them went. And Letitia would have all the rest of New Bedford clued in.

Rollo leapt onto my lap purring raucously. He kneaded my thighs, stepping around and around in his dance swiping my nose with the tip of his tail at each pass.

"You're hungry. Aren't you?" I looked at my watch. "Goodness, it's almost noon."

The detective put away his notebook and pen. "It would be very good if you could come with us this afternoon, Mrs. Rendle. May we pick you up at two?"

"I'll be ready." They made as to leave. "Oh! Mr. Pereira, I'm not a suspect, am I? I mean, if she were uhm—"

"At this point, everyone in New Bedford is a suspect," he answered. But did I see a trace of a smile?

Chapter Three

On the Monday after I had identified my aunt's body, I was putting away the groceries: steak, hot dogs, milk, bread, cat food, and kitty litter. It was almost a week since my aunt's death, but I did not want to meet up with anyone I knew and have to talk about it, so I had driven to Fall River's Shay's supermarket. The same chain grocery was within a few blocks of our New Bedford house, but the extra fifteen miles was worth the gasoline to achieve anonymity.

I thought I heard the kitchen door creak open followed by a soft closing thump. When I turned to look who was there, no one had come in. *Odd*, I thought. A few seconds later, Rollo barged through the kitty door. "You take that right back outside, Mr. Rollo Cat." A little gray short-tailed mammal hung from his jaws. Was it my imagination or did the creature wiggle, being still alive and intended for an exciting toy in a game of chase-around-the-house? Grabbing the broom I kept near the door for such emergencies, I swooshed it at my game-carrying feline. Rollo and vole slipped back outside. I put away the last couple of grocery items, wondering why the kitchen door had seemed to open when no one came in. I stared out the back window, my attention caught by a squirrel skipping merrily from tree to bush; I thought, at least for a few hours while shopping, life had seemed almost normal again. Then the front door opened and shut quickly.

"That you, Steve?"

"Uh huh."

I heard him trot quickly up the stairs and run water in the bathroom.

I laid three pre-made hamburger patties on the broiler. Potato salad from the supermarket's deli, pickles, and coffee would complete the menu. Just as I set the plates on the table, I heard my husband's feet clomp down the stairs. Steve slipped into his chair, looking tidy and smelling of soap and aftershave.

"You smell good enough to eat," I purred, slowly patting the back of his hand and tracing the untanned stripe where he usually wore his grandfather's ring with my finger, the one with the huge blue diamond. He must have left it in the bathroom, I thought to myself. "Don't forget your ring."

Steve scowled. "Got a meeting." He snatched his hand away. "Big Wigs at school."

"But you're on sabbatical."

"Yeah, well, you know how it is." Steve stuffed his mouth full of burger and said no more. We finished our meal in silence like the long-married couple we were. But I was a little hurt by his almost surly reticence. He had been quiet a lot lately, never offering explanations. Steve pushed in the end of his dill pickle with his index finger, licked off his fingers, and gave me a sour pickle peck on the cheek. He picked up his briefcase and dashed out the front door without saying another word.

I cleaned up our few lunch dishes and went upstairs and ensconced myself in my favorite place, our spare room. Right after I sold my first postcards, Steve admitted I deserved a place to do my artwork. This room had become my studio, my room of my own where I came to draw, write, and think. It is on the corner of the house with three windows, two on the south side and one on the east with pale, creamy walls. A bright and cheery, yet cozy place, I loved to be there.

I'd been sitting at my drawing table for a couple of hours, scribbling and trying to come up with some saleable sketches of U Mass Dartmouth I thought would appeal to visiting parents. Crumpled paper overflowed my wastebasket. Neither inspiration nor hard work at sketching produced anything I would want to offer for sale. My artistic spirit was not rising to the occasion.

The occasion was yesterday's publishing of Aunt Sarah's obituary. The police had finally released her body for burial. Detective Pereira had found her daughter "Cookie", whose real name was Maria Katherine Urkhardt of Springfield, Illinois, and located the two grandsons within a few days of their aunt's death. They would all be here for the funeral. Since they were coming a considerable distance and had busy schedules, "Cookie" had decided calling hours would be brief, 6 to 8 P.M. tonight. The funeral would be tomorrow at ten at Aunt Sarah's church. It would be a full service, complete with communion. After the committal at the grave, her friends and family would return to the church for a meal prepared by the women of the church.

Steve's ring was not in the bathroom.

A little later, a soft knock came at the front door; I could just make it out, a gentle tap-tapping. A tentative short buzz of the doorbell followed. That would not be kids playing their doorbell prank. There was never anything hesitant about their cranking of the doorbell. They would probably still be in school. So, I pushed myself from my chair, stretched a little to relieve incipient stiffness in my bad back, and reluctantly left my drawing table. I went downstairs to answer the door.

I peeked out the sidelight and saw an old repainted blue Volvo standing at the curb. When I opened the door, I found Aunt Sarah's timid friend, Marta Jensen, sort of backing off the doormat, as if leaving.

"Why, hello, Marta. Do come in."

The tall, pale-eyed woman's face broke into a shy smile, her ancient weathered face a maze of fine lines and soft winkles. "Well, I just had to talk to you, Annie. I hope I am not interrupting your work too much."

"No, no I was just going to have a cup of tea. Will you have some?" Gesturing for the old woman to come to the kitchen, I saw her chin quiver as she passed me. I put the kettle on and pulled out a chair for her. I put some cookies on a plate.

"How are you doing?" both of us speaking at the same time. After a few more such pleasantries, the kettle sang.

As we sipped our tea, I saw Marta's chin quiver again and her eyes fill.

"Oh, dear, I'm afraid I have a touch of something— an allergy, I think." She fussed in her purse and dabbed her eyes with a lace-edged hanky.

I sipped and waited, thinking if I acknowledged her welling eyes she might burst into tears. Later she'd be embarrassed and ashamed of herself.

Once the handkerchief returned to her purse, Marta sat up straight and drank a little tea. "It's the tea," she said.

I nodded for her to go on.

"I had tea with your aunt the day she died." Then, in a tumble of words, Marta explained how the cops came to question her. She used the word "cops" as if it were a curse word. Normally, my aunt's gentle friend would probably have said policeman or officer. "Now why ever would they do that?" the old Norwegian woman asked me.

"Because I had to tell them who all her friends were."

"Friends? Friends don't kill friends. They came back and fingerprinted me."

I felt a cold wave race like an electric shock down my back. I sat up straight almost leaving my chair. Could Marta have it in her to harm my aunt? To harm anyone? Suddenly, she didn't look so old and frail to me. Perhaps she had a spine of steel.

"Why'd they do that, Marta?"

"I don't know. They kept asking me about what I did that morning. Finally, I told them."

"You didn't tell them the truth the first time?"

"No. I said I was home. I was afraid. But they kept after me." Marta had been a child in Norway when the Nazis invaded her country and she still had fearful memories of the secret police, and police in general.

"You said you had tea. Did you wash out the cups?"

"No."

I remembered now seeing the mugs beside the sink. "They probably took fingerprints from all her friends—until they found a match—yours."

"We argued, Annie, Sarah and I... I came to ask if she'd donate some violets to the Christmas sale—maybe those lovely two-colored ones. She became annoyed and said the women's group was being presumptuous. Then I said I had to ask because the sewing circle had requested I ask if she'd donate something for the white elephant room. Apparently, I made a mistake in suggesting that old quilt she had in her living room."

"Oh, no! You didn't! She loved that quilt!"

"I didn't know that. But then Sarah started to cry and rub her neck and the back of her head. She went out into the living room and pulled off the quilt and held it close to her—ah—person." Marta was nothing if not genteel. "Your aunt then told me to leave because she was getting one of her awful heads."

"A migraine."

"Oh, Annie—I killed her!"

Marta buried he face in her hands and cried like she'd break apart.

I took hold of her shoulders. "Marta, Marta, listen to me. You did not kill my Aunt Sarah. You did not give Aunt Sarah a fatal migraine. She was smothered. Detective Pereira told me."

Immediately, I realized I shouldn't have said that. The detective had told me most emphatically not to discuss the murder with anyone. "Among other reasons, for your own safety. There's a murderer out there."

It took some time before Marta was convinced, if she *was* convinced, of her innocence. Then the old woman fired a volley of questions at me about what I knew about the murder. Bearing in mind what Detective Pereira had told me, I was careful and did not reveal any more facts and satisfied her I knew little, other than finding her on her bed.

Marta finally left, and I returned to my upstairs studio where I found myself doodling eight-pointed stars surrounded by circles, the compass rose design of my Aunt's quilt. It was hopeless to concentrate now on my drawings, so I indulged my racing mind by contemplating whether Marta could be a suspect. Something about her manner when she told me she had lied to the police made me a little wary, and then, now that I thought about it, why did she want to know so much about the murder investigation? Did she want to know how close the police were to catching the murderer? To arresting her? Oh, dear, I hoped I hadn't done anything to help a murderer get away.

My doorbell buzzed again, a loud full-throated buzz this time. Before I could get down the stairs, I heard the front door bang open.

"Yoo hoo! Annie!"

Oh, my God. It was Letitia! Last person I wanted to see was that nosy old gossip. She should have been a tabloid reporter. She sniffed out stories like a bloodhound following a week-old scent from an undershirt. Always wreathed in fluffy violet, lavender, or purple scarves, large clunky bracelets on each wrist and a mound of silver curls atop her head reminding me of a well-groomed poodle; she was tenacious as a pit bull in her search for good gossip. The members of the African violet club, of which she was eternal president, called her "President Pooch" or simply the "Pooch" being too delicate to use the proper term for a female dog.

The unmistakable tomato-y aroma of lasagna teased my nose and tummy before I reached the first floor. Letitia stood in the front hall presenting a large casserole.

"For you, dear."

I muttered the required, "Oh, you shouldn't have!" and led her into the kitchen.

"I'm so sorry, Annie!" Letitia squealed at the top of her lungs. "For your loss, I mean. But she's been dead for a week, why so long before the announcement?" Letitia leaned forward across the kitchen table and peered demandingly into my face.

"Well, the po— the relatives are all from away and it took some time for them to arrange to get here." I was determined not to mention anything again about the murder, especially to the "Pooch." "I believe it was the daughter's idea to have very brief calling hours. She's staying at the Hampton Inn." I hoped that would satisfy her. But no.

She sat back and pursed her lips and shifted in her seat. "Dearie, I'd love a cup of tea."

"I'm out of teabags," I lied and hoped to God I hadn't left the box of tea on my kitchen counter as her eyes flicked quickly around my disorderly kitchen.

"What did she die of?"

"How should I know?"

"Now, Annie, don't be coy with me. The police came to my house, you know. You found her."

Was Letitia a suspect? Would she kill for violets? Nobody would do that. But then if anyone would, Letitia would.

"She died in her sleep, I expect. She was seventy-five after all. Just like you."

That gave her a moment's pause, but just for a moment. She sat back in her chair and adjusted the violet eyelash scarf she had arranged under her powdered jowls and smoothed her lavender heather suit. "Now, Annie, her plants."

"I am watering them."

"They require considerable care," the president of the African Violet Club sweetly purred, obviously implying a mere mortal, and an artist at that, could not possibly give Aunt Sarah's violets the tender care they required. "Now, if you would just give me the key, dearie, I'd be glad…"

"I can look after her plants. I have done so many times."

"She has some rather –er special plants."

"I am up to the job, Letitia. I've looked after her violets several times. Thank you for your offer and for the casserole." I stood and pushed in my kitchen chair. "Now, if you'll excuse me, I have work to do."

There was no way I'd let the eager "Pooch" get her hands on my aunt's new hybrid. Besides, the house had been a crime scene and belonged to the heirs whom I assumed would be "Cookie" and Captain Matthias Spears.

I might not have gotten rid of her even then but for the phone ringing.

"Well, dearie, if you need any help with the plants.…"

"Thank you. See you tonight, Letitia."

I didn't answer the phone until I heard the door close behind her.

"Hello. Yes, this is Mrs. Rendle. What? How can that be? There must be some mistake.

Yes, I'll—ah—ask him about it." It was the secretary from Steve's department.

Then, Steve phoned to say he wouldn't be home for dinner, but his meeting was resulting in good news. He hung up before I could say much.

Strange. I thought. First the college called and asked for Steve, saying there was something about forms for travel allowances for his sabbatical. I was too caught off-guard to tell them he was conducting his research right in this area, traveling no further than Boston or New York, or that he was in fact at a meeting on campus at that moment. Strange they didn't know that.

The phone rang yet again. "Hello? Oh, yes, Mrs. Tripp, I do remember meeting you at Aunt Sarah's. You live next door in the white house with the big front porch. No, it's no trouble. Call me anytime. Well, I'm not surprised. Oh? Really. One of the same men? He did? Oh, he did. Did he get inside? Mrs. Tripp, I really think you ought to tell the police about this. Well, if you'd rather. Okay. Keep an eye out and let me know if you see anything else. And keep your door locked. I know, I know, but just a little peek from behind your curtains should be okay. Good-bye for now, and thanks for calling."

My mind was racing. First the college, then Steve's call, then Mrs. Tripp. And tonight was the wake. I had to settle down. Get my thoughts organized. And get going to the wake.

The first step toward settling down and getting organized was a cup of nice hot tea, my comforting cure-all. As I warmed my hands around a big mug of Earl Grey, I thought about Mrs. Tripp's words and fears. An old woman, living alone and next door to the sudden death of another woman her age, Mrs. Tripp said she was envisioning a mad killer of elderly females. Not likely, I thought, but I couldn't say I blamed her. I had met her only a few times. She was a Yankee of the old school—tall, rail thin, self-reliant, independent, and tough as old boot leather—or at least she usually was.

She told me on the phone, first, the police had come and talked to her last week. From them, she understood Aunt Sarah's death was suspicious. She told them the morning of my aunt's death she had noticed a young man in a dark, suede-like jacket coming around from the back of the house. After the police left, she remembered a few days ago, probably on

Friday or Saturday, she had seen two men outside in Aunt Sarah's driveway. One handed the other some sort of paper, and the other took out his wallet. She thought he gave the first man some money. She couldn't be sure, but she thought one of the men was the same man she saw on Monday. She also saw a little while ago a heavy-set man, looking very furtive, skulking about. He went around to the back of the house, and she thought inside. "He was up to no good," she said. "A real bad one, he looked this way and that before he went around to the back of Sarah's house," she said. He even looked up at Mrs. Tripp's house to make sure no one was looking. She hoped he didn't see her. Now she was really scared. "That man looks dangerous," she said.

She said she called to see if I knew who might have any business at the house. I couldn't think of anyone. This made the poor old woman even more afraid. Now she was afraid to have the police come by, in case some of these bad types were watching the house.

While I thought her fears exaggerated, I agreed to call for her.

But first, but first what? What to do? Eat, shower, call the police? When in doubt, eat.

I'd leave the lasagna for when Steve could eat it with me. I pulled a Hungry Hubby Meal from the freezer and shoved it into the microwave—no way was I settled enough to cook, and time was running short, already after four o'clock.

I pulled out the phone book and looked for the police's number. I flipped through the pages and ran my finger down the numbers for the police department. So many choices. Everything from domestic abuse to—wait a minute. I think I have a card from Detective Pereira. I slapped the phonebook closed and headed upstairs to my bedroom intending to search my purse and pockets for Detective Pereira's card. I'd make that call, then jump in the shower, dress, and head for the funeral home. I was halfway up the stairs when a vision of Aunt Sarah's violets popped into my head. Lordy, it had been how many days? Too many.

Chapter Four

I grabbed my purse, ran downstairs, and was locking the back door when I heard a familiar jingling. Was that the telephone ringing? Blast! I'd let it ring. They would probably leave a message. Feeling utterly pressed for time and uncertain how I'd ever get properly dressed and to the funeral home in Fairhaven, I reversed out of the driveway and just missed a passing car.

My stomach squished into a knot and my heart pounded. With every muscle tensed and my heart in my throat, I drove the car at snail speed to the corner, taking stock of my quivering insides. *Yes, I'm all right. Heart slow down, please.* God hadn't wanted me to die today. I must have had an angel on my shoulder. I took a deep breath. Three deep breaths. *I'll just drive over and see to*

Aunt Sarah's violets. They are really her living legacy. If I don't get to the funeral home, so be it. I don't want anything whatsoever to happen to her dear flowers.

A few minutes later, I pulled into Aunt Sarah's narrow driveway. A curtain fluttered in the first-floor window of Mrs. Tripp's house and the light went out. I stepped from the car and walked around to lock the passenger side so Mrs. Tripp could have a good look at me and waved to the curtained window. I thought I saw the white lace quiver.

Good girl, Mrs. Tripp. You are keeping watch.

I hurried down Aunt Sarah's minuscule driveway and past her old black Ford Fairlane sitting forlornly in front of the two wooden garage doors that slumped on rusted hinges. She never used her ancient one-car garage, and I had no idea what was in it.

Three straggly rose bushes stretched across the back fence of my aunt's tiny patch of yard. A few late blooms dangled from their spidery canes. In one corner stood a cement bird bath, dry. In the other corner, the nearly empty birdfeeder drooped from a dispirited old apple tree. A cardinal flew past my face in a dreadful hurry, it seemed, to reach the birdfeeder ahead of the squawking blue jay on the garage roof. I paused a moment to see whether the cardinal or the jay would demand a place on the feeder. The blue jay won. How much my aunt had loved all of nature's creatures. I choked back a sob then scurried up to the house.

A screened porch added at some point in the old house's long history ran across its width. I had a key to my aunt's back door, but the screen door on the porch was always held shut by a hook on the inside. Before going up the three steps to the porch door, I looked under the pot of basil my aunt kept at the bottom of the steps. Nothing. Then I lifted the pots of thyme, marjoram, and lastly parsley.

Where was that thin little butter spreader my aunt kept hidden under these pots to slip between the screen door and its frame to unhook the door? I ran up the steps hoping to rattle the door open. As I pulled, it flew open so easily I nearly fell back down the steps. Mrs. Tripp was right. Someone had been in this house. It was someone who knew where that little knife was kept. Almost immediately, I saw the butter spreader lying on top of the birdseed can. Then I saw the footprints. They led to a clean, dust-free rectangle on the porch floor and back to the screen door. Someone had removed the large toolbox from the porch. At least I thought it was a toolbox because I remembered Aunt Sarah saying it was a box of old tools that was her husband's or belonged to one of his friends. I really must call the police.

I twisted the key in the lock and was inside in a jiffy. To my right were pegs with coats, an old flannel shirt, and the big canvas apron my aunt wore when repotting her violets. Ahead of me was a door to her vast old-fashioned kitchen I loved so well, and to my right the door to the corner room where the violets grew in an effulgence of purples and pinks. They all looked happy, seemingly not having missed their mistress. There, against the far wall overlooking the driveway, was the bi-color: a soft creamy blossom tinged with a rosy salmon. The plants did not seem particularly dry, but I set about watering and tending as I had so many times before, following the schedule on Aunt Sarah's clipboard that hung by the door.

Twenty minutes later, I headed home. Rollo met me at the front door. Bird legs lay on the doormat. I was in too much of a hurry to do more than mutter, "Bad cat," as he slipped between my legs and ran inside. The message machine was indeed beeping. Steve.

"Uh, Anna, is tonight the wake? I'll be there, but I'll be late. I have something nice to show you. Love ya, bye."

I deleted the message and ran up the stairs. I tore off my clothes and jumped into the shower long enough for a once over splash. Dressed again, I found my purse and fumbled through it until I found the detective's card. Our old grandfather clock downstairs bonged six times. I was already late for the wake. Dialing Pereira's number, I was told he was out, and asked if they could take a message. I gave them my cell phone number.

Rollo gave me a major ankle rub as I searched for where I dropped my keys. "No time to feed you, cat. Besides, you are probably full of bird."

"Please, Lord. Don't let the bridge be open." The bridge across the harbor was an ancient drawbridge topped with four purely decorative pointed Victorian finials.

On a schedule known only to God and itself, the bridge would swing aside to let New Bedford's fishing boats go out to sea. Luckily for me, it behaved itself and in ten minutes I was pulling up to the funeral home on Washington Street.

I had to park in the street. As I pulled the funeral home door open, a young man in a black, three-piece suit came to greet me. His dark, pomaded hair was molded to his head in a style reminiscent of his grandfather's day and he tugged nervously at the cuff of his shirt as if the sleeve was too short. I placed him as one of the younger Robinson brothers, the family who ran the funeral parlor. He indicated the guestbook with his hand and a somber, but shiny, white-toothed smile.

As I signed, he stage-whispered, "Oh, but you are part of the family. They are looking for you." Steering me by my elbow, he led me to the front of the room where two young men dressed handsomely in preppy-looking V-necked sweaters, pale blue shirts, navy sports jackets, and gray slacks stood with a stolid, severe middle-aged woman to whom the usher introduced me, calling her Ms. Urkhardt; she was Aunt Sarah's Midwestern daughter.

She scowled at me as I tried to whisper away my lateness but told me I was to call her "Cookie" as she pulled me around to face a mourner coming down the receiving line. It was Mr. Jepson, my aunt's lawyer.

After thanking him for his expression of sorrow, I had my first opportunity to glance at my Aunt Sarah as she lay in her coffin. She seemed to glow. Rosy cheeks and petal pink lips reflected the undertaker's art more than my aunt's taste in makeup. From the corner of my eye, I saw the same pink on Cookie's lips and knew from where the undertaker had taken his cue. Of course, it was Cookie who had made all the arrangements. She was the chief mourner, after all. Still, I had always felt so close to my aunt, saw her several times a week, but rarely heard her say anything about Cookie.

I mumbled my way through a string of Aunt Sarah's sewing circle friends, the pastor's wife, and several strangers, one of whom, a pimple-faced teenager, introduced himself as "her favorite bagger at Shay's market." Every chance I could, I'd sneak a peek at the door hoping to see Steve come in. No Steve.

The crowd was thinning out. It was about quarter to eight when I glimpsed familiar faces standing outside the room. It was Per Pereira and his partner Joe Rodriques. I tried to catch Pereira's eye. Did he nod my way? I could not be sure because just then Steve hurried into the room. He paused before my aunt's casket, standing with his hands folded in front of him. I saw his shoulders shake and his hand reach out and touch the edge of the casket. He stood there, looking so tenderly at Aunt Sarah's body. My heart went out to him. I had no idea my aunt's death had affected him so deeply. Finally, he took a deep breath and exhaled slowly, squared his shoulders, and tugged at the hem of his sports jacket. He turned toward the receiving line, nodded at the two grandsons and Cookie, and came straight over to me.

"Oh, Steve." I reached out and placed a hand on his chest.

"I'm sorry, Annie. I know I should be standing here with you, but I just can't. Let me just wait outside. I do have something to show you." He patted his breast pocket.

"Of course, dear. I understand."

Steve pulled out a big plaid handkerchief from his inside coat pocket and blew his nose noisily, wiped it left and right. He squeezed my hand and retreated to the hallway.

I thought I saw a hand reach to him and pull him aside, but just then the doorway was mostly filled by a big shambling man who wore a green Celtics jacket and stained chinos. Even in this age of casual attire, he was very much underdressed for the occasion. At first, I thought he was a homeless person, seeking warmth from the cool autumn evening. But he came straight up to the casket, knelt, and crossed himself.

After a moment, he stood. I saw his lips move and heard him whisper, "Oh, Sari, Sari, you was so good." The big man stood there a moment more. Then he sniffed and wiped his cheek with the heel of his hand. He gave his thick paw first to one grandson and then the other. His voice rumbled, "You must be the grandkids. She talked about you a lot." Then he approached Cookie.

"Katherine Urkhardt, her daughter," she said, nodding and smiling tightly, but not giving him her hand.

"Joe Brown."

I gasped.

He looked up at me.

"Oh, dear, I'm sorry," I mumbled, "but, but I think I met you once, at my aunt's house. I'm sorry I didn't recognize you." I didn't know if I blushed red or blanched white. I was so nervous. The detective had implied Joe was our chief suspect.

His big, brown, droopy, hound dog eyes seemed to look right into my soul. "Anna, right?"

I nodded.

"I have something for you. After the funeral. In a few days." He hung his head and shuffled out.

I saw Pereira pull him aside.

Suddenly, the soft music stopped and lights dimmed. Startled, I turned to look at Cookie.

"The visiting hours are more than over," she said and explained she and the funeral director had agreed this would be the signal for the last stragglers, as she called

Aunt Sarah's friends, to leave. "I like things to run smoothly. Stay on schedule," Cookie added as if for my elucidation before I could say anything.

The two grandsons paused before my aunt's coffin for one last goodbye. One placed his hand on the satin coffin lining. His Adam's apple bobbed, and I heard him whisper, "Good-bye, Grandma." The other wedged his fist against his mouth in his effort to keep back tears. I could see his eyes were glistening. Cookie took both young men by their elbows and steered them out.

I stood alone with my aunt in the silent, darkened room. I didn't know why, but I said, "Aunt Sarah, what happened?"

The quilt, Anna. The thought was forceful and seemed to be her voice. I looked one more time at that sweet, old face and, batting back tears, made my way into the hallway.

I looked around for Steve. Nodding toward the restrooms, I asked the funeral director if my husband was there, but he, of course, didn't know Steve.

One of the Robinsons went into the men's room to check for me. "No one is there," he said when he returned. "Oh. Thank you. I think he must be waiting for me at home."

Before leaving, I conferred a minute with Cookie about tomorrow's funeral. Lastly, I talked with Detective Pereira, who was waiting inside the door about Mrs. Tripp's observations. He promised to keep a close watch on the house.

The bridge was open. A big fishing boat, a scalloper, plowed slowly through, heading out to sea. So, I had fifteen minutes to mull things over before the two sets of wobbly railroad-crossing-style gates would swing up and a stoplight would turn green to let the two lines of traffic through.

The whole time Joe Brown's words kept playing in the back of my mind. One minute, I was seeing him as a murderous thug. He sure looked disreputable. What did he have for me? If he really were the murderer, did he have a knife in the back for me? Or was it a little pressure on my neck from those two huge thumbs? Was that what happened to my aunt? Then again, in my mind's eye, I'd see his droopy, sad eyes with their red rims, how he really seemed to grieve before Aunt Sarah's coffin and think, no, that big lug wouldn't hurt a fly. Again, there was definitely something criminal about that man. And Steve? Dear Steve. How upset he was! I would never have expected it. Showed you never really knew what a person thought, I guessed. And what did he want to show me?

The light flicked to green and slowly the line of cars, trucks, and buses began to move through.

Chapter Five

As I approached our driveway, I saw Steve had pulled his Cherokee only halfway up the drive and left it at an angle at that. Now, why had he done that? He was usually so particular about his driving and often gave me a piece of his mind over my careless parking. In parking lots, I was too close to the white line on one side, or too crooked, or hadn't straightened my wheels. I'd become very self-conscious about my parking. Parallel parking was almost beyond me at this point, but now I had to park on the street.

He must have been really upset about Aunt Sarah's death or something else. I had no idea what, but I was beginning to think there must be something else going on. What was the reason for the misplacement of his ring? His gruffness? His lateness several times and his deeply emotional behavior at the wake?

As I stuffed my keys into my purse and pushed open the door, I heard a weird little clatter. I heard it again as I walked into the kitchen.

"Rollo!"

Rollo had the look of utmost innocence on his face; his eyes glowed with astonishment. His empty food dish was overturned in the middle of the kitchen floor. He sat with his paw on his water dish and was going to tip that over as well when I came into the kitchen.

"Okay, okay, I more than get the message." Quickly, I snatched the water bowl and scooted it back into his feeding corner next to the refrigerator. I fumbled around in a drawer and pulled out the can opener. Rollo rubbed around my ankles, purring raucously. His body language proclaiming I was his best friend, not the cold-hearted, abusive parent he claimed I was a minute ago. The purrs and ankle rub-arounds worked their magic; I gave him an extra-large serving.

Now I went looking for Steve, pulling off my coat and setting down my purse in the front hallway.

"Annie! That you?" called my husband in a hazily slurred voice from the living room. He was slumped in the big easy chair, one foot on the ottoman and the other askew on the floor as if tossed aside. I joined him, sitting down on the edge of the couch. He held a tall glass half-filled with something amber colored. A nearly empty bottle stood on the floor beside the ottoman.

"I needed a drink."

"Steve, I'm sorry the wake was so hard on you. I had no idea."

"Yeah, the reality of it all got to me, I guess. Bad."

"Perhaps you should stay home tomorrow. You don't really need to come to the funeral."

His face brightened momentarily. "We—ell, I do have some new sources to check out. You know, on my poets of early New Hampshire. It's a poor excuse, I know, but my sabbatical is flying by. Next semester, its back to teaching."

"*Seems to me it had always been poets of early Vermont, a comparison with Robert Frost,*" I said to myself. "*Yes, I know it was,*" I remembered seeing that on his sabbatical application. I had typed it. The nearly empty whisky bottle strongly suggested this was not a good time to discuss this with him.

Suddenly tired of it all, I too wanted a drink. It had

been a very long day. I reached over and took a little sip from his glass. Ooph! Whisky, neat.

Steve sat up straight in his chair, cleared his throat the way he did just before he lectured his classes. I had taken *American Literature* from him for my teacher's certificate and remembered that little half-cough and ahem. Back then, I thought it was cute. Tonight, I thought bad news was coming.

"Ahem, Annie, 'member I said I had something for you? Us, really. This has been so hard for you, losing your aunt." He pulled something from his pocket. "Well, I had some luck with Gerry and the guys." He held up a brochure; a very colorful one.

I leaned forward to see it better. "Aruba—where happiness lives," it read.

"Honey, we are getting away!"

"Oh! Wow!" I was so excited. I'd never been out of the country, let alone to such a romantic place. "Oh, Steve, you're wonderful! So lovely." I leaned over to kiss him, but instead sank into the couch, immediately deflated. I remembered our nearly empty bank account. Moving back onto the ottoman, I caressed Steve's ankle and reached again for the whisky, then decided against more of the strong stuff. "Uh, Steve, how *ever* are we going to pay for such a trip?"

"Now, honey, don't you worry your pretty little head about that. I've worked things out with Gerry."

I hated it when he talked about my pretty little (read: empty) head. *Don't patronize me!* I screamed internally, but not wanting to start the argument, I let the patronizing issue pass.

"We'll be on that plane as soon as you can pack," grinned Steve, a silly whisky smile spread across his face.

"Not for a while. That detective said he may have more questions for me and wanted me to stay in town."

Steve's smile vanished, and his eyes took on a strange hard glint. He picked up his glass and drained it. "Damn! You are always so hard to deal with!" He stood and flung his glass toward the fireplace. It hit an andiron. Shards of glass flew across the floor.

I heard a rapid *thump, thump, thump* and saw a frightened Rollo racing upstairs.

"Cat's got the right idea. Let's go up to bed."

It took a while, but eventually I persuaded Steve to come to bed, that tomorrow would be a better day, and we'd talk it all over then.

Thunder woke me. Rain pounded the roof, more like the hammering in of three penny nails than a gentle patter blessing the ground. Rollo snored on Steve's pillow, happily curled into a ball; a catnip mouse lay beside him.

"Steve? Where are you?" Pale morning lightning flashed against the bedroom curtains. I grabbed my bathrobe and checked out the bathroom. Another roll of thunder, not so loud this time, drummed behind the raindrops. His toothbrush wasn't there.

Confused, I hurried down the stairs with Rollo running interference between my ankles. The coffeepot was on in the kitchen and a dirty mug sat in the sink, along with a plate, a butter-smeared knife and the heels of jam toast.

"Steve?"

He was not in the living room. He did not appear to be in the house. Maybe he couldn't sleep and went for a walk. Then I saw the note. Just a few scribbled words ending with: "I'll call in a few days. Love ya."

That man! I thought, *so good at teaching students; so bad at communicating with wife.* Early New Hampshire poets, bull! Where was he off to now? I cracked two eggs into the pan and along with three rashers of bacon and toast, *I* would have a substantial breakfast. Doggone it! It would be a long, busy morning and not a pleasant one.

First, still in my bathrobe, I cleaned up glass from around fireplace. Then I got out the vacuum and gave the living room a thorough vacuuming. I didn't want to leave even the most minuscule piece of glass behind that might get into Rollo's paw. I vacuumed the cat hair off the couch and chairs and then quickly dusted the furniture, all the time working over in my mind what Steve could possibly be up to. Had he won a large pot playing cards with "the boys"? Could we really go to Aruba? But hadn't he just said he was under pressure to get his research done before his sabbatical ended? And what to make of his strange absences? Another woman? Our love life had not been exciting lately. But, no, he wanted to take me to Aruba. I could come to no conclusions except something was wrong.

After my micro burst of cleaning, I took a long, luxurious shower and then wedged myself into my slightly tight, rarely worn, navy suit. The funeral was not until ten. The newspaper was out on the lawn, but practically soaked into the grass. I did not even try to bring it in. The rain still hammered down, so I went up to my studio to pass the remaining time. I sat musing and doodling on a pad of paper. When I looked down at my scratchings, there it was. Plain as day, the circle and star design from Aunt Sarah's quilt. My pen had unconsciously drawn it three times. Kind of like magic. Scary! A chill ran down my back. Was that a message, or what? I crumpled the paper and tossed it toward the wastepaper basket. I missed. Picking it up, I saw the design again. Now I really felt there was some sort of message there, but what?

Grandfather bonged in the downstairs hallway. Time to get going. I drove to the church. The bridge was open to cars. No boats wanted to go to sea just then. I found one of the few remaining slots in the old wooden building's parking lot. As soon as I entered the church, one of the Robinson brothers greeted me and said I was to walk in with the family. He showed me to a side chapel that had a stained-glass window depicting Christ walking on the water. A pale sun glowed pink and gold through a mariner's compass rose in the top most pane. Later, I noticed all the uppermost window panes in the church had the same compass rose. Appropriate for a seaside church where many of the men were fisherman.

I sat next to Cookie. She nodded to me and alternately dabbed at her eyes with a crumpled handkerchief or scrunched the cloth between her hands in her lap. It seemed we waited an eternity before I heard the organ music swell and one of the funeral directors escorted us into the narthex of the church.

Pastor Sven, a white-haired former navy chaplain, moved down the center aisle, tall and erect as a flag pole. The coffin, covered with a pall, followed him pushed on a gurney by two Robinson brothers. Honorary pallbearers followed, including Aunt Sarah's grandsons. Cookie walked behind them, and I followed. The family took the front pew on the left.

During the first hymn, I glanced around. The church was full. Aunt Sarah's friends from the African violet club, in their dark purple finery, filled the first few pews on the right-hand side. Letitia was prominent in a broad-brimmed black straw hat with a purple silk rose pinned to the band. Behind me sat the old ladies of the sewing circle. Marta at the end of the pew looked shriveled as if trying to disappear.

The pastor intoned: "Out of the depths have I cried unto thee O Lord…"

"Oh, God!" a man cried from the back of the sanctuary. Sounds of scuffling. "He promised he'd be here with the dough! That bastard! Let go of me."

Pastor Sven hesitated, then continued with the liturgy. "Let thine ears be attentive to the voice…"

Then the scuffling and shouts and curses disrupted everyone. I stood to see. In the back of the church, the two Robinson brothers and Detectives Pereira and Roderiques struggled with two huge, dark-haired men. Pereira twisted the arms of one man behind him and handcuffed him. It was not half a minute before it was over. The two men were escorted out of the church. Silence hung heavy in the sanctuary.

After a moment, the pastor nodded to the organist and she began to play. It was then, just before I reclaimed my seat, I saw Joe Brown amble into the sanctuary and sit in the last pew. He bowed his head.

The long funeral procession began with the hearse. Behind it, the flower car followed, then a pair of black limousines, a number of SUVs, and even a couple pick-up trucks, proving my Aunt Sarah had been a very popular lady indeed. As a family member, I was shown into the second limo with Cookie. The two nephews rode in the first with the other pallbearers. The string of vehicles wound its ponderous way across the bridge and into the city, through streets narrow and wide, stopping the traffic at intersections. Finally, we passed through the stone arch that was the gateway to the cemetery. After a few turns through the park-like grounds thick with granite slabs in remembrance of the dead, we came to a halt.

As I stepped from the car, robins bobbed across the wet grass. One pulled out a worm. A gaggle of geese honked and yakked high overhead, going who knew where. And the sun came out. The nephews and the other pallbearers lifted the coffin from the hearse. The casket rocked once when one youth used his hand to wipe away a tear. The Robinson brothers had placed the coffin over the grave by the time I reached the graveside.

A gentle breeze ruffled the flowers that lay across Aunt Sarah's casket. As I took my place next to Cookie and Pastor Sven opened his little book, brown leaves rustled on the oak trees.

"My quilt, Anna. Yours."

No, it must be just the leaves, the wind, I thought, a ghostly wind. But it certainly sounded like her voice.

After the commitment ceremony, the mourners made their way back to their cars, but I stood there. I couldn't leave yet. Leave her. A tear ran down my cheek.

Cookie turned back and whispered to me, "Come. We should be going," and she turned on her heel and walked toward the waiting cars.

One of the grandsons put his arm across my shoulders and gave me a tentative gentle kiss on the cheek, whispering, "Take your time."

Aunt Sarah was gone now, really gone. I stood a few moments more until someone touched my elbow.

"May I help you, ma'am? It's best you come to the car now," a Robinson brother spoke gently, but firmly.

We all went back at the church's fellowship hall. The sewing circle ladies, who were also the bereavement committee, had lain out a huge meal. While my brain didn't want to think of anything festive, it was almost noon, and to my amazement, my stomach was crying out for food. Wonderful fish and quahog chowders donated by fishermen's wives, cold cuts, baked beans, an array of potluck casseroles, luscious looking cakes and pies. I had always wondered why funerals were followed by a meal. But then, at least it gave you something to do with your hands, and it seemed too soon to talk, I mused as I carried my plate and sat next to Cookie and Sarah's two grandsons.

After I had finished my food and was drinking a cup of coffee, Mr. Jepson, my aunt's lawyer came up to me.

"As I told Ms. Urkhardt, Anna, there will be a reading of the will at my office tomorrow afternoon at two P.M. You should be there."

Cookie and I agreed to meet for lunch the next day before going to the lawyer's office.

The next morning, Wednesday, I was cleaning up my breakfast dishes when the front door banged open.

"Steve! Where have you been?" There was an odd faint oily smell about him. I couldn't place it.

"Boston Public Library. Got a lot done. Need to take a shower." He bounded up the stairs, without so much as a peck on the cheek for me. He looked like he'd been up all night. When he put his mind to something... Just then, the phone rang. It was Letitia.

"Mr. Jepson's office is on fire. Wasn't he Sarah's...?"

"Yes, yes. I'm sorry, Letitia, I have a call on another line." I did. I didn't need to lie to the old gossip. It was Cookie with the same news. We talked for a minute but agreed to keep our lunch date.

I threw some clothes into the washer. The phone rang. It was Detective Pereira.

"Mrs. Rendle, is your husband at home? I'd like to speak to him."

"He's in the shower." I could hear the water running.

"Could you see he doesn't leave the house? I'll be over within half an hour. Those men at the church yesterday were looking for your husband, Mrs. Rendle.

They have criminal records to the moon and back. I feel your husband may be in danger." He rang off.

The phone rang yet again.

"Hello? Oh, hello, Mrs. Tripp." My heart sank. Not more bad news. I didn't think I could take much more. But, alas, Mrs. Tripp's behind the lace curtain spying had produced results. She had seen two men go around the back of Mrs. Spears' house and lights go on inside.

"When?"

"This morning before six. I'm an old lady; I don't sleep that much. Please tell the police—you know how I feel."

"The detective just called; he's coming over here, Mrs. Tripp. I'll tell him."

I hung up before she could ask why Pereira was coming over. Why *was* he coming over? I wasn't sure. Mechanically, I smoothed out the afghan on the back of the couch. "Quilt," a voice in my head said. I sighed. *Please, Lord, no more voices*, and fluffed the toss pillows on either end of the couch. Then I took the cover off the cat-hair free chair for the detective to sit on. *Goodness, I wonder where Rollo is. I haven't seen him this morning. I hope nothing has happened to him. No, no, he is probably out birding or mousing.*

The phone rang. A deep voice rumbled, "Anna, this is Joe."

"No! No! Please, I don't want to talk to you now. I can't." I slammed down the phone. A murderous end or a million dollars, whatever he had for me, I couldn't handle Joe Brown now. Not with Steve acting so strangely, my aunt just buried, and all these phone calls coming at me.

Then the doorbell buzzed with an angry clamor. Everything all at once. Oh, dear God! I ran my hands through my hair; I'd about had it.

The doorbell buzzed again, and the cat flap rattled in the kitchen. Rollo pranced in and jumped up on the cat-hair free chair. He plopped a huge blue jay on the seat, its limp neck smeared with congealed blood. But the yucky carcass saved the moment, for just then Steve came thumping down the stairs wearing his "I'm-in-a-big-hurry scowl" and carrying his briefcase. I knew he'd head out the door if he could.

"Er—dear, could you get the door?" I asked, scooping Rollo up under one arm and pointing to the door with my blood-smeared feathered-filled hand.

The bell rang a third time and a fist pounded the door. "Police!"

Chapter Six

"Okay, okay, I'm coming. Hold your horses!" Steve yelled and opened the door.

Pereira and Roderiques pushed their way in, silent and stone-faced.

By the time I returned from throwing the dead bird into the kitchen garbage and had scrubbed my hands, the three men were seated in the living room. I heard Pereira ask:

"Do the names Manny Frates and Joe Riley mean anything to you?"

"No."

"Well, they should. They are Gerry Ramona's enforcers," snapped Pereira.

"Your poker buddy, Gerry?" I blurted, totally surprised.

Steve jumped up from his seat. "You shut up, Annie. Stay out of this. Get out of here. Don't you have some cooking to do or something?" He took me by the shoulder and gave me a shove toward the kitchen.

From the corner of my eye, I saw Officer Rodrigues step forward, ready to intercept.

"It is not a matter of a friendly poker game, Mrs. Rendle. Your husband has acquired vast gambling debts. Frates and Riley would have collected at the funeral or put your husband in the hospital."

I reached for the little desk chair behind me. I had to sit. I could not stand up. My heart pounded against my chest. Tears were about to burst from my eyes. So that was why he was so upset at the wake that he couldn't make the funeral. A big act to avoid payment or worse. I sniffed and battled back the tears.

"Steve, what is this? When you said you had some luck with Gerry and we were going to Aruba, I thought you had won in poker."

"I sold my ring and leather coat," Steve mumbled, looking at the floor. To the cops, he said, "I don't know these guys. I don't know what you're talking about."

"I would like to think you didn't, because if you did, I'd say you need GA counseling really bad, pay what you owe, buddy, and watch your back. Mostly this last, Mr. Rendle. Be very careful. And keep us informed if you go out of town. We still have a murder investigation underway."

I couldn't begin to describe the next two hours. The crying, the shouting, the whining, the agony of realizing my whole marriage was a fraud. I may now be a penniless, what? Bum? Also, the detectives' parting words had sent chills up and down my spine. Were we both still suspects? I rushed at Steve. I wanted to sock him and would have if he hadn't grabbed my arm and pushed me onto the couch. My insides were shaking, and I felt so much tension in my arms and legs I thought they would burst. Why hadn't I at least insisted on access to the checkbook? Why had I let Steve so run my life? I always let him have the last say. Why? Why? Was it because he was seven years older than I was, or because of his many years of education? Well, no more! I resolved, as he got out the whiskey bottle and handed me a glass of amber liquid. Okay resolution, where did I start? Could I take a sip and mellow out and still be firm in my intention to stand up for myself? I took a tiny sip. The liquor burned warmly in my mouth and seared its way down my throat. I felt a pleasant flush, but my brain kicked in telling me this was not the way to handle this situation. What to do? Independence wasn't learned in an instant or from a bottle.

Talk about saved by the bell. The telephone rang once again, halting further discussion or fighting. I made Steve answer. I just couldn't.

He handed the receiver to me and growled, "It's Cookie." Because Mr. Jepson's office was a burned-out black hole, she wanted to change our luncheon date to a meeting with him at her motel.

By the appointed hour, two P.M., I had showered and applied globs of make-up to make my tear stained face somewhat presentable. It would take all my presence of mind to get through this meeting. I certainly didn't want Cookie to know of Steve's gambling debts.

Mr. Jepson was prompt. The Hampton Inn let us use one of their small conference rooms and a housekeeper in a crisp white uniform set a pot of coffee on the table, along with some thin vanilla wafers. Mr. Jepson sunk into his seat. "I don't know why this happened. I'm just a moderately successful lawyer, no high-powered clients. Mostly wills and deeds. It's arson, the cops say." He poured some coffee gesturing to offer us some.

I took half a cup just to have something to do with my hands. Cookie took none.

"I'm afraid your aunt, Anna, has now died intestate. She was odd about some things. Of course, when she came to make her will—this was few years ago—she had no thought of dying so soon. I clearly remember her saying she did not want a copy to take home or put in a safe deposit box. I think the only copy was in my office safe. After the funeral, I had pulled it out and left it on my desk to read to you. And my papers were burned." He paused and looked off into the distance. "Arson. I guess the lawyer needs a lawyer." After a moment he continued. "Anna, I do know that your aunt had made some provision for you in her will. I don't remember just what, but without the will, I am afraid her heirs will be her children, Mrs. Urkhardt here and the Captain. And there will be considerable time in probate."

The lawyer talked for some time with Cookie; I listened with one ear, lost in thoughts about my aunt and Steve. Thinking of Steve's problems and his increasingly almost violent behavior, and my own impulse to clobber him, brought me to wonder if I might not need Mr. Jepson in my life. He seemed to be of an equable temperament even in the face of the loss of his office.

My attention was brought back to the matter at hand when I heard their chairs scraping as my cousin and the lawyer stood. Mr. Jepson was my aunt's executor and Cookie seemed eager to get back home. It was agreed, for the time being, I should look after the violets.

Just as we were walking to the door, Cookie touched my arm and said, "Anna, if there is something you'd like, some little thing to remember your aunt by, I'm sure I wouldn't mind." Her tone suggested it had better be a "little thing".

"Oh, I don't know." Then it came to me. "There is one thing. Aunt Sarah had a quilt I liked. It's just an old quilt. Would you let me have that? A compass rose quilt she had made," I added, and then regretted I said that. It might make the quilt sound valuable or something.

But, no, Cookie immediately said, "Compass rose, violets, or petunias, I don't care much for home-grown folksy stuff. My house is all Louis Quinze." She actually put her nose up in the air. "Sure, help yourself." Then her eyes narrowed. "I'll go with you now." She, of course, wanted to make sure I didn't take anything else from her "estate". We set off in my car.

"You know, Cookie, Aunt Sarah often spoke of me having her quilt," I said as we turned a corner. That was not strictly true. My aunt had indeed mentioned me having her quilt a time or two, but I could not honestly say it was often. However, the voices in my head, in the wind, in the trees, and in the tossed pillows certainly came often enough.

"I'm sure then she meant for you to have it," Cookie charitably answered.

As we pulled into my aunt's driveway, I remembered suddenly what it had been that was wrong when I saw the quilt covering my aunt when she was dead. She had always kept it on the back of the couch in the living room, never on her bed. I wondered why someone had covered her with it when she died, was murdered. Then I remembered Marta. Had she put my aunt to bed? Covered her with the quilt? Or just left. And if not Marta, who?

Cookie opened the front door with the keys Mr. Jepson had given her. A damp air surrounded us, and a chill crept around my shoulders and down my back. This was the first time I'd come into the house by the front door since that awful day. The heat was turned down, yes, but it was more than that. Memories rushed over me like ghostly spirits and one of them was definitely evil.

We stood in the hall until Cookie finally said, "Well, where is your quilt? I don't want to take a lot of time here."

"I want to just take a peek in here."

I stepped into the living room and turned on the lights to sort of chase the damp spirits away.

Cookie sighed, frustrated. "Anna, I really don't want to spend time here in this awful old house."

The quilt was not on the couch, but I could make out a darker, less faded rectangle on the upholstery where it had lain. With heavy heart, I trudged up the stairs to her bedroom and paused outside her door.

"Standing here is not going to change anything," murmured Cookie. "Let's get this over with."

She opened the door and with a quick prod between my shoulder blades thrust me into the room. The bed was stripped bare to the mattress.

"The forensic people," Cookie assured me. "Is that your quilt over on that chair?"

I hugged the old comforter and buried my face in it. It would need a good airing, I thought, it smelled like death.

"Okay, let's go. Let's get out of here." This time it was me hurrying my cousin out the door.

I put the quilt on the back seat and as we drove away, Cookie began an explanation of her haste. "I'm sorry to be in such a hurry, but I've already made plane reservations. I've so much to do, and I must see Mr. Jepson once more before I leave. I've been away from home much too long. Twelve days is too long to leave my business."

"Twelve days?"

"Yes, I was in Boston when the police informed me of my mother's death at a decorators' convention. I'm thinking of going into home decorating along with real estate."

She practically leaped out of the car when we got to the Hampton Inn, calling out, "Good-bye. Nice to have met you!"

Driving home, I had a chilling thought. *In Boston, was she? She could easily have come down to New Bedford and gone back with no one seeing her. She was awfully eager to get her hands on my aunt's estate. I wonder? Nah, no daughter would do such a thing, but then… Oh, I don't know.*

I pulled into my driveway, no Cherokee. And the mess my own life was in came back to sock me in the face and send cold shivers down my spine. I plunked my head against the steering wheel and sat in the car for a few minutes biting my lip and fighting back tears. I dragged myself into the house.

This time he had left me a long note. He was at the school. He would eat supper in the college cafeteria and spend the night in his office. He had brought a sleeping bag. He needed the quiet to think. I was not to worry, he said. He figured he was safer there from "enforcers" than at home, at least for tonight. I could call him, if I wanted, but was to use the cell phone. He loved me, he said, and would call in the morning.

I sat at the kitchen table thinking. Well, at least I knew where he was. But, boy, did we have issues—as his students would say. Perhaps a cooling off period was for the best. I really didn't want any more discussions, fights, or whatever right now. Still, I couldn't help wondering constantly what would happen. Would we have to sell our house? But that was surely jumping the gun, wasn't it? But, oh, I wished I had kept up with our finances instead of letting Steve do it all. How did this all begin? He was so busy with his research. When did Steve do all this betting? How could he concentrate on his research with so many problems? His research? What did I really know about it? He did not discuss it with me. I had always assumed he thought I was too ignorant and uneducated to know anything about it. I was not to trouble my pretty little head. Maybe there wasn't any research. Maybe he was placing bets right now. That thought turned my stomach. I picked up my cell phone and called his office. No answer.

Our grandfather clock bonged seven times. Goodness! How'd it get so late?

I made some supper—tuna fish salad sandwiches— and was sitting with my cup of tea with Rollo sitting on the table next to me, purring and washing his face; he had had his own plate of tuna, and right now I needed his furry company. The doorbell buzzed.

I had the door on the chain. A huge figure filled the opening. Joe Brown.

"Anna, can we talk?"

"Now's not the best—"

"I didn't kill your aunt. Ask the cops. They'll tell you."

Somehow those sad puppy eyes got to me and I let him in. *In for a penny, in for a pound,* as my mother would say.

"Would you like some coffee or tea?" I asked holding up my mug of tea. My hand was shaking a little.

"Tea would be good. It's what she always gave me."

"You had tea with my aunt?" I found that unbelievable, this rough uncouth lug and my classy aunt.

"Yeah, she was real good to me." He plopped his heavy frame down at my kitchen table and was silent until I set a cup of tea before him. "Cops say I'm the only one with an 'unassailable' alibi. I think that means a good one."

I almost smiled. Did Joe Brown have a dry sense of humor or was he really uncertain of the meaning of the word? The latter I realized as he continued.

"I was at work. They keep a close watch on me. And me, I know when they follow me. I got certain talents. But I'm keeping real clean."

His words confused and frightened me. "Whatever are you talking about? Where do you work? What are your talents?"

"You're fast with the questions, Anna."

I squirmed in my seat. "So much is happening," I murmured.

"Sari and I was friends." He went on as if he hadn't heard me. "She once said I should look after you."

"What?" I nearly screamed.

"Yeah, and you're gonna be more surprised when you hear me. I work at Shays' Market in the back loading, unloading. Heavy work, where no one can see me."

"Why where no one can see you?"

Joe was quiet a long time, sipping his tea as if considering whether he should tell me. "Sari didn't tell you?"

"No. My aunt never said anything except you were an old friend of my uncle's." I wasn't comfortable with him calling her Sari. It was as if he was closer to her than I was.

"Okay." He took a deep breath, let it out, and began to talk, almost as if he was out of practice. "I did seventeen years in the big house...for armed robbery." He sat back to see how I took this news.

I had a criminal sitting in my house and I was alone with him. It took me a minute and several tries, opening my mouth and shutting it again. At last, I spluttered, "But my aunt seemed to like you."

"Yeah. Your uncle and I was buddies in the army. When they came to put me away, some of my stuff was with your uncle." He drank some tea and then continued. "I've been out of the slammer some two plus years and, believe me, I don't want to go back. I'm keeping squeaky clean. When I got out, I came to get my stuff. Your uncle was dead, but Sari was good to me. Gave me a room for a week and persuaded the manager at the market to give me employment. I had nuttin'." Another pause. "My parole officer was some surprised I had real work and kept m' job. They really don't think any con can go straight."

"But you do want to?" I asked in a timid voice, giving myself time to absorb this new information.

"Let's just say I seen the light."

We were both quiet for a minute. Then I asked him, "Joe, when I went to water the violets, I saw a box was missing from the porch. And footprints. And the neighbor said some big guy had gone around to the back of the house."

"Yeah, me. Sari had found more of my stuff and put them out there. Mostly tools of my former trade. The coppers came again and asked me about what that neighbor lady saw."

I was glad to know the police were checking out Mrs. Tripp's information. I got up and put a plate of cookies on the table. Joe munched hungrily.

"Joe, you must know about as much about the investigation as I do, and I don't know much. Who do you think killed my aunt and why?"

"Why is easy. She had heaps o' cash."

I was astounded. But Joe convinced me. When he lived there, he had seen a financial advisor come to the house. Apparently, my aunt was a very savvy investor and it was kind of a game with her.

"But who?"

"Wasn't you in the will?" He gave me a penetrating stare and then a smile. "And no, I don't have that great an alibi."

Then we talked over Cookie's rather odd behavior and decided she could use some looking into. Then I told him about the arson. If that was related to the will, then we thought it had to be someone who'd inherit, will or no will. That left only Cookie and my aunt's son, really. I thought the grandsons unlikely. Joe just shrugged, muttering something like "Ya never know." Cookie had been in the area for some time and was now hurrying back to Illinois.

Then Joe surprised me. "Unless there is another will. You have keys to the house. Who else did?"

"Nobody I know of. Unless a neighbor."

"Anybody could get in that house. I could get in in a minute."

"Is that one of your talents?"

Joe laughed heartily. "Yeah, but I'm twenty years out of practice."

We talked some more. By the end of the evening, we had a sort of unspoken partnership. A sort of trust had developed between us. We had exchanged life stories, with the exception of Steve's current troubles.

"You said you had something for me, Joe, what is it?"

"Oh, some kind of bone thing your aunt was fond of. I didn't bring it 'cause I wanted to see what you was like first. Whether you'd be understandin' or not."

"Well, there is something more I must share with you, too. But I want to wait until next time. I need to sort things out a little with Steve."

Joe sort of grunted and got up from the table. Seventeen years in prison, I figured, made him good at keeping his own counsel. We agreed we'd meet to search Aunt Sarah's house for another will or a copy of the one she'd left at the lawyer's office.

Joe had no car. He had walked a long way to get to my house. "I'm saving for one. My credit's not exactly good. Gettin' a pre-owned in a couple days." He laughed a deep rumbly laugh.

I drove him home and then sped out of that nasty south end neighborhood as fast as I dared.

Chapter Seven

The next morning, I called Steve again. He was okay, he said, despite spending a restless night in his sleeping bag on the hard, cold floor of his office. He hadn't realized the college turned the heat down to fifty-five at night. "Saving your tax dollars, ha, ha," he joked lamely. I asked if he wanted to come home for a hot breakfast. He said no, he felt he'd be safer eating at the cafeteria. He didn't want any of Ramona's enforcers to see him driving to and from the house and follow him to the school. In a few days, I could come and collect his dirty laundry and bring him fresh clothes.

I felt a little like a well-trained dog and had a mental picture of myself bounding up the college steps with clean underpants in my mouth.

I went on to tell him about meeting and talking with Joe Brown. At first, he didn't like me having anything to do with Joe Brown. He thought he might be working for Gerry Ramona, until I told him I had met him at my aunt's house many months ago.

When I said he was a former burglar, Steve really didn't like the idea of me having anything to do with him. "For all you know," he said, "he may be worming his way into your confidence so he can rob you."

I had to admit that was a possibility, but I didn't think so because Aunt Sarah had trusted and let him in her house many times. Steve then mumbled something about how I had only Joe's word on that. But when I told him he had come up with the idea of looking for a second copy of the will, instead of being angry, as I expected him to be, he actually brightened.

"Great idea," my husband said, "I'd go with you myself except I'm kind of on a roll here with the poets. Gotta go with the creative flow, y' know." He seemed to have forgotten for the moment he was in hiding, called me "good girl", and cheered me on with "way to go." I agreed to stay in touch and snapped my cell phone shut.

I next called Shay's for Joe. He had started work at the loading dock at five A.M. and would be done at one.

I'd pick him up, we'd have a bite to eat, and go to my aunt's house.

As we pulled into my aunt's driveway, Mrs. Tripp's curtain flicked. When I got out of the car, she pulled her curtain completely back and gave me a big smile and wave, but the old lady's eyes opened wide, horrified when Joe got out on the passenger's side.

"Our informant is on duty," I said to Joe, laughing and nodding toward the neighbor's window.

Joe didn't think it funny.

We went in through the back door. I walked straight through the kitchen into the front hall where I tapped the thermostat up to sixty-eight and listened with satisfaction as the old oil burner rumbled into action.

"Where to start?"

"Where she did her writing," Joe reasoned.

"I once saw her paying bills in the kitchen. She had a little writing desk in her bedroom and there's an old secretary desk in the living room."

"Okay, I'll take the bedroom 'cause you probably don't wanna go in there, ya know, where it happened. You do the kitchen, and then we'll try the living room if we need-ta."

I happily agreed with that plan. Joe pulled off his jacket and flung it over the newel post as he started up the stairs. I heard something in his jacket pocket clunk against the post. It sounded like a rock. I was chilly and kept my jacket on until the house warmed up.

Even now, my aunt's kitchen was a bright welcoming room; I recalled the wonderful smells of baking bread so often greeting me when I came by for a cup of tea. The walls were painted a pale yellow and wallpaper featuring nesting chickadees covered the wall nearest her plant room. I decided to be methodical about my search and begin at one end and open every cabinet and drawer. A quick open and shut of the upper cabinets revealed canned tomatoes, spaghetti sauce, green beans, and jars of peppers. The first lower cabinet held a huge canner, its lid with the pressure gauge laying upside down inside it. The drawer above it held a jar lifter, a wide mouth funnel, and three boxes of canning jar lids.

The next cabinet was full of small pots and pans of various sorts with lids crammed in at various angles. The drawer above this door held can openers, slotted spoons, some jar openers, and a church key. I worked my way through several more cupboards and drawers each chock full of gadgets and pots. My back was complaining when at last I finished and straightened. It was then I saw the long row of cookbooks on the counter and knew my work there was far from done. Stuffed amongst them were all sorts of pamphlets and papers crammed in hither-skitter between the pages. I sighed at the thought of going through all of them, as I must. I could hear Joe upstairs opening and shutting doors and pulling out drawers. *God! He's going through Aunt Sarah's clothes—all her undies, everything!*

Then I noticed a long narrow drawer and pulled it open. It was full of mail, bills, letters, bank books, and pens.

"Jackpot!" I thought this had to be where something important was. I felt a little overwhelmed with a ton of cookbooks and a drawer of papers to go through, when I heard Joe come galumphing down the stairs.

"Nuttin'," he said and sat at the table and rubbed his eyes with the heel of his hand.

"I've just found a huge bunch of stuff to go through."

I put on the tea kettle and began piling cookbooks on the table. Twenty minutes and a cup of tea later, we'd been through all the books. The papers were mostly recipes, "receipts" as my aunt called them. Mostly they were for food, but some home remedies were thrown in as well and even some little poems and bits of advice from some newspaper's "Dear Agatha" column.

"Yuck," grumbled Joe, "here's how to make horehound cough drops. My ma used to make those. Tasted awful."

The drawer full of papers required more tea and took an hour. It was all business stuff including bills, seven letters, fat bank books, and two checkbooks, but no will. I put the letters aside to read later thinking they might be informative. At last, we moved into the living room.

While I was pulling open the drapes to let in some light, Joe exclaimed, "Well, what do ya know? Like we was meant to find it."

When he pulled down the drop-leaf front of the secretary desk, a fat envelope slid out from a bunch of papers. On the front was typed "Last Will and Testament of Mrs. Sarah Spears". I reached for it, but Joe pushed my hand away.

"I got a funny feelin' about this." He reached into his pocket and drew out a pair of thin, black, cotton gloves. "Fingerprints, ya know."

We went into the kitchen where the light was stronger, and Joe carefully pulled the will from its envelope and spread it on the table. He wouldn't let me touch it. It was a store-bought form for people wanting to make out their own wills without the expense of a lawyer, perfectly legal if properly signed and witnessed.

I read. I could not believe my eyes.

"If your jaw drops any farther, it's gonna fall off."

"Joe, I don't believe this. She left me so much: the house and contents and money—so much money."

"See if it's signed."

"Letitia and Marta witnessed it. They never told me!"

"Probably sworn to secrecy." Joe slid the will back into its envelope.

"Cookie let me have Aunt Sarah's quilt, which was all I ever would have wanted from her, but this... This would... Joe, you don't know how much this means to us."

I sat on my aunt's sofa and told Joe the whole story of our debts and Steve's gambling habit.

Joe listened without saying one word. "They say, 'Don't count your chickens...'" was the only thing he said when I had finished. "But this is so wonderful. I knew Aunt Sarah was fond of me, but I never thought she would leave me so much. If she had as much money as you suggested, that still leaves plenty for her son and daughter. Ten thousand plus the house will solve all our problems."

"They also say, 'If it seems too good to be true, it probably is.'"

I slumped into the couch. "You're right. I shouldn't get excited yet. What do we do now?"

"Call your lawyer."

I scrounged in my pocketbook and came up with a business card for Mr. Jepson. Yes, he would see us. He gave us directions for his house. It was in Marion.

"Before we go, I just want to check my aunt's violets."

Joe went back the down the hall for his jacket and slung it over his shoulder. "Oh, yeah. While you're excited, I should give you this. Your aunt seemed to think it special." He pulled out a curved hunk of ivory and handed it to me. It was a six-inch long sperm whale tooth scrimshawed all around with pictures.

"Oh, thanks, Joe." I stuffed it in my bag. It was nice of my aunt, but I'd look at it later.

"Your aunt said it was special," repeated Joe giving me a hard look.

I pulled it out again. On one side was carved a ship under full sail. *Rosalind* was inscribed round the base of the tooth twice; once below the ship, and once below the voluptuous Polynesian lady on the reverse. She wore a palm leaf where she had to and nothing else.

"No wonder you thought it special," I giggled.

"I said your aunt thought it special," Joe sounded sour. "I got good money for them things even when they wasn't real. This one's real."

A little chill passed down my spine. Even then, I suspected this might be my aunt's real legacy. Shame-faced, I stuck it back into my bag and mumbled I'd take it to the whaling museum and see about it.

In the plant room, everything seemed at first to be fine, sun-filled and steamy with moisture. I set to work with the watering can. Rows of cheerful plants smiled their pinks and purples at me as I made my way to the end of the little greenhouse. But when I looked for the hybrids, just two brown rings of dirt marked the shelf where they had sat. Where were they? Panicked, I ran along all the shelves looking for the salmon-colored plants my aunt had cherished. I looked under the shelves and tables behind bags of potting soil and stacks of flower pots, everywhere. They were not to be found.

"Everything else seems normal. Someone came in and stole them."

"Who'd steal posies?" wondered Joe as we backed out of the driveway.

"Someone from the African violet club," I blurted. "Letitia thought they were pretty special. That woman…if she—" I shut my mouth. As upset as I was, I couldn't believe Letitia would stoop to that. But what were we to think? All Aunt Sarah's acquaintances, retired burglars aside, were genteel ladies. At least I had thought so. Surely none of them would break into the house. What was even more confusing was apparently no one had actually broken into the house. Joe checked all the doors and first floor windows before we got into the car. No one had made any use of Joe's kind of underworld talents.

It was after four when we arrived at Mr. Jepson's house. His home was a stately but elderly white clapboard house on Water Street.

"Classy digs," Joe whispered under his breath as we ran the bell.

After a second ring, a tall silver-haired woman came to the door. Hardly moving her mouth, she asked, "Yes?" She glanced at me, then Joe, and back to me. "I don't think we need anything."

Quickly, before she could shut the door, I said, "I'm Anna Rendle. I'm looking for Mr. Mark Jepson, my Aunt Sarah Spear's lawyer. And this is my friend, Joe Brown."

"Oh, yes." A tight smile broke across her face, sending up rows of wrinkles over her cheeks. "Terribly sorry, but it's been an awful time. My husband's just been with the police—the arson, and then he twisted his ankle. Please, do come in. He's here in the living room."

She led us into a large room where tall front windows paned with old wavy glass let in the last of the day's light. A ruby and royal blue Persian rug covered most of the floor. Mr. Jepson sat in a wing chair by a flickering fire with his foot up on a cherry coffee table.

"Please, make yourselves comfortable. Excuse me for not getting up," he said with a gracious nod toward me, "I'm rather pinned here. Can we get you something? Some coffee?" To Joe's almost imperceptible nod, he turned to his wife. "Eleanor, would you bring us some coffee, dear?"

I introduced Joe and explained about the second will.

"Well, let's see it." He read it over quickly. "Seems to be alright." Then he squinted at the witnesses' signatures and began reading it over again; this time more slowly. Eleanor came in with a tray and setting it down on the coffee table next to her husband's foot, chortling a little as she urged him to be careful with his foot and not knock the coffee pot over. She made a great production of pouring coffee, offering cream and sugar, and passing around a plate of cookies, crackers and cheese. It being so near to supper time we both helped ourselves to food and drink. We thanked her, and she discreetly left the room.

"You say your friends never told you about this?"

"No."

"I'm sorry, Anna. You are not an heiress. I don't think this will is valid."

"What? Why?"

"According to this, your aunt left Letitia Marston, Marta Johannessen, and Priscilla Bronstad legacies of a $1000 each. And the same Letitia and Marta witnessed the will. A witness cannot legally be a beneficiary of a will. Imagine the mischief that could be..." He stopped short as he remembered Sarah Spears had indeed been murdered.

"Let me call Letitia right now and get to the bottom of this." I plunged into my bag after my cell phone. I tossed out my wallet, the whale tooth, and my car keys before I got to the phone.

Mr. Jepson called Eleanor back to the room. He asked her to make a photocopy of the will.

Letitia wasn't home. I did not have Marta's number in my phone. I put my wallet, keys, and so forth back into my purse. We all stared at each other for a moment or two. Finally, Mr. Jepson folded the original put it back into its envelope and handed it to me.

"I think you'll want to show this to the police. It may have some bearing on your aunt's untimely demise. Ahem." He cleared his throat. "I'm very sorry, Anna. Please don't hesitate to call me if I can be of any service. Forgive me if I don't see you out." He lifted his foot momentarily from the coffee table.

We both stood. I reached over and shook the lawyer's hand as Joe fumbled with the zipper of his Celtics jacket.

"Add fraud, makes four," Joe muttered as he pulled up the zipper and started for the hallway.

"Four?" Mr. Jepson and I both asked.

"Yeah, you didn't tell about the posies. Murder, arson, the phony will, and missing violets." I told Mr. Jepson about my aunt's new "posies."

"Well, I definitely think the police should look into that also. Could be the motive."

"My aunt killed for her violets?"

"People have killed for less," both men said simultaneously.

I looked from one man to the other. My knees felt like water. Eleanor's food rolled around in my stomach.

I pressed my hands against my stomach, pulled myself up very straight, and took a deep breath. Perhaps I swayed little, but I was okay.

"I had hoped there would be no more police." Even as I said it, I knew the police had a long way to go before all these crimes were solved. I saw the two men look at each other, man to man. Mr. Jepson nodded, and Joe took my arm.

"Come on, Annie. The man's done all he can for now."

I figured I was being hustled out before I got weepy. I was determined not to be a hysterical female, making a scene. But, right now, it felt good to be taken care of, on a man's arm. As soon as we got outside, and the crisp October breeze hit my face, I felt better.

"Sorry, Joe. I'm okay."

"Course you are, kiddo. Let's get some supper."

We went to the Pasta House, Dutch treat. We ate spaghetti and had spumoni for dessert.

It was quite dark when I pulled into my driveway. Service at the Pasta House was slow and, of course, I had to take Joe home. But I could see a white patch on my kitchen doorstep. Rollo. What was he doing out? He could go inside any time he wanted through the cat door. As I walked up to the door jingling my house keys, my beloved cat gave my legs the old rub around treatment. As soon as I stepped into the house, I realized I had forgotten to feed him. My punishment was his water bowl tipped over and its contents pooled across the floor. I could not be angry with him. It was what I deserved. He was the best-behaved part of my little family now. What was a few dead mice between friends? He didn't gamble, acquire debts, or run off chasing Vermont/New Hampshire poets. Grabbing a couple of paper towels, I mopped up the mess before hanging up my jacket. Then I cranked open his favorite chopped grilled chicken and liver dinner and humbly placed it before him. I sat at the table and watched my furry friend chow down.

As Rollo washed his face and ears, I got up to make me a cup of tea. It was then I saw there was a phone message. Steve had left three messages all to the effect of "Where the hell are you? Call me. I want to know about the will."

I picked up the receiver and then put it back down. "I need a drink," I said to myself and worked my mind through a series of thoughts from *never drink alone* to *just for medicinal purposes*. Half convinced I had a scratchy throat, I splashed a dollop of Steve's whisky into my tea along with a little honey and a cinnamon stick. I curled up on the couch with a steamy hot toddy. I'd call Steve in the morning. *Also,* I thought, *it is rather late to call Detective Pereira. Tomorrow is soon enough for the police as well. The will is probably not important.* Then I remembered Mr. Jepson had said something about motive. *Yes, I suppose the fake will is important, maybe very important.* I sipped and thought for several minutes. And the more I sipped, the more I thought there had to be a connection between the will, the motive, and the violets. Remembering the stolen violets, I wondered if Marta or Letitia would have killed for the violets and a $1000 legacy. It didn't seem enough to kill for. Maybe they hoped to use the money as an investment in an African violet business. Nah! That was silly. But the arson. That was not silly. Nor was it a lady's crime. Someone could have been killed. Was there a man involved? Some old guy might be attracted to Letitia's high maintenance fluffiness. I giggled as I thought of Letitia's violet suits, lavender scarves, and plum polished nails. Yeah, she was spectacular.

I drained the last of my hot toddy and was feeling pretty tired and a little hazy from my drink. Well, sometimes I did my best thinking in bed. I started up the stairs and slipped on the second step. I grabbed the railing in time to keep from stumbling. I chuckled to myself as I could hear my mother saying, "Never drink alone." This time she added for good measure, "even for medicinal purposes." I drifted off to slumber-land and saw Letitia's purple-painted fingernails scoop potting soil around an orange violet, and Joe Brown tear recipes from my aunt's cook books, crumple, and throw them to the floor muttering in that low, rumbling voice of his, "Nuttin' here, nuttin' good." I heard a door slam and Steve stride in demanding I find his leather jacket.

I sat up fully awake. Where had I last seen Steve's jacket? And why was it important? I was sure it was important, very sure. Dreams had a way of telling truths. It was 2:30 in the morning. Sliding beneath the covers, I rolled over and turned back to face the bedside table with its digital alarm clock glaring at me. I could not get to sleep. An hour passed. I kept thinking I must look for that jacket, maybe not right now, but surely in the morning. I rolled onto my stomach. Rollo stomped into the room as only a cat could when a cat wanted to stomp. With a little chirrup, he landed on the bed and snuggled against me. Soon his purring and the rhythmic pricking of his needle claws against my blankets had me dreaming, this time of cans of tuna fish and can openers.

Chapter Eight

It was almost eight o'clock when Rollo's heavy-footed jump onto the end of my bed and his subsequent tramp over the length of my body woke me up. Grandfather bonged downstairs as I pried my eyes open. Golden sunlight streamed in through half-drawn shades. I really hadn't been paying attention when I went to bed last night Good thing my neighbors' view was blocked on that side by their big, former carriage house of a garage.

"Okay, okay, kitty cat. I'll get up and feed you. You are not going to starve this morning."

I tumbled into the shower and let the hot spray pelt my shoulders. Then toweling off and giving my hair a quick once over with the blow dryer, I tugged on jeans, a turtleneck shirt, and a heavy sweater. Pulling my hair back under a headband, I scuffled into my fuzzy slippers. By this time, Rollo was yowling like a banshee for his breakfast.

Downstairs, Rollo tucked in to a bowl of dry cat food and then some chicken and liver feast scooped from its overpriced miniature can. I made myself a huge breakfast of home fries, bacon and eggs, toast, and coffee which I ate slowly, wanting to put off the unpleasant phone calls to the police and to Steve. It was going on ten when I pulled out my cell phone and dialed the detective's office. I was told he was out. Then I tried Steve. No answer. I left a message.

I had slid the last plates into the dishwasher when my cell phone rang.

"Hi. Sweetheart!" *Hmm the nerve of him. Sweetheart was it?* "I was on the highway when you called. Lot of cops on the road today. So I pulled into the service area at that Burger King, you know, where you got sick that one time?" My husband chuckled.

"That was not funny."

"Yeah, well, I didn't want any overzealous cop pulling me over for distracted driving."

"Good idea, I guess."

"Listen, honey, I'm heading up to Burlington to track down some old references."

"Burlington!" I screeched. "That's a distance. What ever happened to computers? Google. Y' know?"

"These aren't on any search engine. I'll be back tomorrow late. I'll call. Then you can bring me some clean duds. Okay? Bye." He hung up before I'd told him about the will.

I wanted to say something like, "Up yours, buddy!" I was so upset with him these last couple of days. This gambling debt business and his mysterious uncommunicative behavior really had me thinking about our future together. I gritted my teeth as I clicked off my phone. It wasn't what I wanted for my life. No way! I was just getting started on my own interests and projects—my drawings. I thought maybe I was already getting stronger. I didn't know, but I would not let Steve wreck my life!

I stomped up the stairs to my studio and began drawing with fervor. In an hour's time, I had a dozen views of the U. Mass campus. All pretty good, I thought. With a little refining, they might all be saleable. Amazing how anger could energize.

I was about to break for lunch when I heard that voice again. That urgent whisper: "Quilt, Annie. Look at the quilt." Was it a voice from the other side? Or just a thought that popped into my head? Whatever it was, it was a far more pleasant thought than Vermont poets or gambling debts. Just thinking of Steve's affairs made my stomach tighten. I set aside my paper and pens and went downstairs.

Aunt Sarah's quilt lay across the back of my sofa. So far, Rollo, using whatever passes for feline reasoning, had not been interested in sitting on and covering it in cat hair. Standing in front of the sofa, I lovingly stroked the old coverlet smooth, enjoying texture of the minuscule ridges and valleys made by the quilting. Each quilt block seemed to have its own personality. As my hands worked their way to the bottom edge of the quilt, I felt a soft crinkling feeling. Odd! It was as if paper had replaced the batting. Aunt Sarah wouldn't have been that sloppy when making a quilt. She was so meticulous with everything she'd sewn. I ran my hands along the quilt. The crinkly feeling extended along most of the bottom eight inches of the quilt. She would never have done that.

As I straightened and rubbed out the stiffness from my back where I had injured it long ago, I realized I didn't know for certain if my aunt had made the quilt. I didn't remember her ever saying so. Perhaps it was handed down to her. I squinted over the stitches. They were so tiny and evenly spaced. That didn't tell me much. It could have been machine sewn or handstitched. If handstitched, it was certainly old, but it may still have been made by Aunt Sarah. I smiled to myself as I remembered a story about a woman joining a quilting group. She worked hard, but when she left the other quilters pulled out all the new woman's work because they considered her stitches too large.

I was going to pick up the quilt to check the underside, when I heard a car pull up outside. One then two car doors slammed. I ran to the front windows and peeked through the curtains, thinking it might be Gerry Ramona's enforcers and I'd lock the front door. It was the police.

"Good morning, Mrs. Rendle. May we speak with your husband?"

"My husband?" I was surprised. After all it was *my* aunt who had been murdered, not his. Then I remembered the gambling. "Is this about Gerry Ramona?" Maybe it was good news. Maybe Gerry and his thugs smacked their car into an overpass abutment and were all dead. For a moment, it sounded plausible.

"May we speak to your husband, Mrs. Rendle?" Detective Pereira was stern, his eyes cold and penetrating. Officer Roderiques stood just behind him, hands on hips, his mouth pressed into a grim slit. There was no good cop, bad cop here. They were both bad cops, or so it seemed.

"No. Actually, he is not here."

"Where can we find him?"

"I don't know."

"What do you mean, you don't know?"

"This is not a game, Mrs. Rendle," Roderiques snapped.

To his credit, the detective gave him a sharp look.

Tears came to my eyes. I batted them back and asked the two policemen in. "Look, after I found out about the gambling—you were here then—things haven't been too good between us. Anyway, Steve felt he'd be safer from Ramona at his office at the college. He's sort of been camping there."

"You have his number there?" Roderiques flipped open a notepad.

"Yes, but this morning he phoned me he is on his way to Burlington. Something about his research. He's on the road."

"He wasn't supposed to leave town. We'll track him down."

I gave the police Steve's cell phone number as well as his office number.

"Get it," whispered Pereira jerking his head toward the door, and Roderiques went outside.

"Mrs. Rendle, does your husband have a leather jacket?"

"Yes, it's right here." I opened the front hall closet. "Oh, no, it's not here."

"Does this look familiar?"

Roderiques pulled a filthy jacket reeking of gasoline from a bag. One sleeve was slashed.

"Oh, that thing smells. Can't be his. Put it back, please." I held up my hands as if to push the jacket out the door.

Instead, Roderiques pulled the collar back revealing the initials embroidered inside the neckband. SMR. "Does this help?"

"Oh, my God! Yes, those are his initials. Stephen Mark Rendle. Oh, the smell! Please, put it away." I grabbed my stomach and lurched back into a chair.

Roderiques took the jacket back to their cruiser.

"What happened? Where'd you find this? What is going on? Please tell me!"

"I'm sorry, Mrs. Rendle. We have to ask your husband a few questions."

I could not get more information from them. With a curt, "I'm sorry to put you through this," from Detective Pereira, they left.

I was still sitting on the little desk chair, wiping a stray tear from my cheek with the heel of my hands, when I remembered. The will, the violets, I had tried to call Pereira about them. He was out, they said. He must have been on his way here, maybe. I yanked the front door open and dashed to the sidewalk waving my arms over my head and shouting, but I was too late. I saw only a brief flash of red and blue lights rounding the corner.

Our old grandfather clock called out twelve times. It was time to eat something. I cranked open a can of spaghetti-rings. Rollo ran in at the sound of the can opener but turned on heel and departed through the cat door at the tomato-y pasta smells. *What should I do? What can I do? What do I want to do? What was I doing before the cops came by? The quilt, yes, I was looking at the quilt. But, Lord Almighty, the cops are out looking for Steve, my husband! I should call him.*

I jumped up and ran to the phone. Or should I? Would I be helping him run from the law? He was already running from the law. Just as I put my hand to the receiver, I heard my cell phone ring in my purse.

"Hello? Steve! I was just going to call you."

"Annie, you gotta come. You gotta help me." His voice seemed muffled, hesitant each syllable formed slowly, as if it took all his strength to speak.

"Steve! What is it? What's the matter? What's happened?"

With sobbing gasps and heavy breathing interrupting his speech, Steve managed to convey something about Gerry Ramona, the car, and where I should meet him.

Dropping my phone back into my purse, I reached for my coat but then immediately hung it up. Steve said he had no money for food and it would be well into the afternoon before I reached that little crossroad of a village. Perhaps I should bring him something to eat. I had no idea how far we'd have to drive to get to a restaurant up there.

I made a pretty mean tuna fish salad, if I do say so myself. Stuffed between whole wheat bread, a couple of sandwiches would hold him fine, I thought. As I walked into the kitchen, I stepped on some kind of crunchy, wiry string. Rollo looked up from washing his face with round-eyed innocence, as if to say, "So, you expect me to throw my leftovers in the garbage? Recycle it yourself!"

Holding the half-gutted mouse by the tail with thumb and forefinger, I made a speedy dash for the garbage pail. I ran the water in the kitchen sink until it was good and hot and using soap and a nail brush gave my hands a good scrubbing, all the time muttering, "Yuck! Yuck!" I started some coffee and chopped up a little onion and celery and mixed them with the tuna, some mayo, paprika, and a few sliced green olives, my secret ingredient. I loaded the sandwiches and a thermos of coffee into the car along with a map and backed out of the driveway.

A ratty old VW square-back crawled past me as I backed into the street. The driver beeped his horn and waved. But not recognizing the car or seeing the driver, I kept on driving.

For two hours I battled heavy traffic pushing my way northward. It seemed like everyone on the road was mad. My middle finger popped up more than once. But maybe it wasn't the traffic on the road so much as the traffic in my mind. What was the trouble with my husband? Why didn't he want to tell me "the worst of it" as he had said over the phone? Who had killed my aunt? Who had stolen the violets? Why was there a false will? Who had gotten into the house to place a will and steal the violets? Was it the same person at the same time? Or two people at the same or different times? And the quilt. Why did I keep thinking my aunt was trying to send me a message from the other side? What was the crinkly stuff inside it? My mind was going eighty miles an hour and the spaghetti in my stomach rolled around at about the same speed.

When I reached Nashua, I pulled off at Exit 4 for a restroom stop. It felt good to sit for a minute in a car that wasn't moving. As I hauled myself out to head for the McDonald's, my knees were stiff, but I had purposely parked a good distance from the restaurant door so I'd have a chance to stretch my legs. As I dodged incoming and out-going autos of all sizes, breathing in the chilly exhausted-laden October air, I found myself thinking, *Be thankful for small blessings—all your limbs are working just fine*. It was something my Aunt Sarah had once said when I was recovering from my back injury. Thinking of her brought tears, and I fumbled for tissue as I made my way to the ladies' room.

Back in my car, I unfolded the map to find the little town where Stephen was waiting for me. I had set my finger down on Route 3 when two police cars went flying down the highway with lights flashing and sirens screaming. They'd found Steve!

I squealed out of the parking lot and followed. I kept them in sight. Then the traffic got heavier and I had to slow down. Two huge SUVs passed me, and I could no longer see the police cars. The right lane had slowed to forty mph. The possibilities in the left lane looked better, so with a quick look over my shoulder, I slammed down the turn signal and butted my way into the left lane.

After a few minutes, the cars in the left lane also slowed down too. I was behind a humongous SUV and completely lost sight of my police cars. I poked along grinding my teeth. After another mile or so, I saw what the hold-up was. The two police cars were parked in the road trying to hurry gawkers by as an ambulance pulled out across the median strip and screamed toward Nashua. Two cars had collided somehow, and one was blackened and steaming where the fire truck was dousing it with water. Water running red spilled across the road. A second ambulance started to move out, but slowly. There apparently was no need for it to hurry. For a second, I remembered the ambulance that carried my Aunt Sarah to the morgue. I knew why this one was going slowly.

Once past the accident, the traffic picked up speed and I flew along looking for the exit and little town where Steve was. Soon I was winding along narrow twisting roads in the countryside. There it was! The small mom-and-pop store and lunch room with tables out in front for eating outdoors in the nice weather. A man sat on one of the benches, hunched down with his head on the table. Could that be Steve? Could that be my husband? That wreck of a human being?

I pulled into the parking area. Got out and looked around for the Cherokee; I could not see it anywhere. As I got out of my car, a plump elderly woman hustled out from the building.

"Are you his wife? He wouldn't let me call an ambulance or the police. Kept saying his wife was coming."

"Thank you, yes. Here, Steve, I brought you some..."

He lifted his head and I saw his mouth was bloodied. I tried to sit him up, lifting under his arms. Steve moaned. It was almost a howl. He slumped back down on the bench.

"Oh, my God. Wait, I'll get the car."

I drove the car over the grass to the picnic table. The old woman had waved for her husband. With him helping Steve up, and myself supporting him under his other arm, we walked Steve, like an injured football player, to the car. The man's wife ran up with a vanilla frappé for him to suck through a straw. "For energy," she said and gave me directions to the small hospital in the little town. It was several miles from their store.

We stopped for gas at a full-service station. While the attendant pumped fuel and washed my windshield and back window, (they really meant full-service), I tried to feed Steve a little of the tuna sandwich. I ate one half and broke off a tiny corner and stuffed it into his mouth. He moaned again. I could see he shoved the bread into one cheek, chewed, swallowed, making an awful face. Then said it tasted like blood, tasted like iron. He wanted no more.

"It's the hemoglobin in the blood. Your gums must be bleeding badly."

God only knew why I came out with that piece of trivial information at the time. Perhaps to restore some sense of normalcy, give us some perspective, or maybe I was just asserting myself, preparatory to having to take on more responsibility for our lives. Anyway, I gave up trying to feed him, paid the attendant, and pulled onto the highway.

Steve's groans were incessant. I could hardly bear thinking of his pain. How I wanted this wretched ride to end! But it had started raining and a strong wind was blowing autumn leaves across the road. I saw a car ahead skid on the wet road and slowed to drive more carefully and arrive safely. I found the local hospital readily enough, but two ambulances had already pulled up ahead of us to the emergency room door. I helped Steve out of the car and as we were hobbling towards the double glass doors, they slid open and a nurse came out with a wheelchair for him. Immediately, they swept him into a back room while I gave the particulars at the desk: insurance, yes, cause of injuries? I wasn't quite sure of the cause or what I wanted to tell them, but I suspected it was a fight, so I told them he was mugged. I sat down to wait and after what seemed an eternity a doctor came out to speak to me.

"Mrs. Rendle?"

"Yes?"

"Your husband seems to have some severe contusions around his chest as well as damage, bruising, to his mouth. He may possibly lose several teeth. He may also have a concussion. I think he should stay overnight for more observation," said the doctor matter-of-factly. He continued, "He really should have some x-rays of his chest. He is getting very groggy from shock, cold, and hunger. I would like your permission to have him x-rayed. However, our technician will not be back until tomorrow morning."

I gave my permission for him to be admitted and immediately said, "We're from Massachusetts. Where will I stay?"

"The folks at the front desk can give you some information on places to stay. We have some very nice bed and breakfasts here in Plankville Village and a small motel not far, about ten miles from here."

I followed the nurse and orderly as they rolled Steve down the corridor and into a four-bed ward. Curtains were drawn between the beds, but I could see the patients as Stephen was rolled toward the bed furthest in and on the left. The nurse snapped the curtain fully around his bed. I heard my husband grunt and cry out as they shifted him onto the hospital bed as I stood in the middle of the ward staring at the shifting bleached pink drapery around Steve's bed.

"Hey, it ain't that bad, is it, buddy?" came a young voice from behind me.

Startled, I spun around, and my eye fell on what

appeared to be, from what I saw of him, a white ghost of a kid in his early twenties or late teens. Without thinking, I blurted out, "What happened to you?"

"Laid down m' bike under a truck," then added, seeing my obviously uncomprehending scowl, "Motorcycle accident." The youth had a bandage, bloodstained, around his head, both arms swathed in gauze wrappings, and one leg in a cast and elevated by some sort of pulley arrangement.

I was trying to think of what to say when the orderly poked his head out from Steve's curtains and said, "We'll be a few minutes, ma'am. You can take a seat outside in the hallway." It was not a suggestion but a statement.

I walked out of the ward passing the other patients in the first two beds. Both were extremely aged. One, much grizzled, slept with his toothless mouth gaping like a black pit. The other, livelier, pushed his glasses up on his nose with his middle finger and lowered the magazine he was reading, but not before I got a glimpse of its nature, definitely a "gentleman's rag".

"Hello, honey. You certainly improve the scenery around here."

I mumbled, "Good evening," and scurried into the hallway.

Plopping down on the chair, I pulled out the last of my tuna fish sandwiches. As I finished off the food, I heard the rattle of curtains being pulled back, the soft plod of the orderly's footsteps followed by the almost silent tread of nursing shoes.

"You may see Mr. Rendle now."

I pulled around a straight-back chair and sat facing Steve. He looked awful. Bruises appeared all over his face. Steve would be x-rayed in the morning, and then we would see where we went from there.

"Honey, I'm sorry, sorry I got you into all this," my husband struggled to say.

"Me, too. I'm sorry too."

"Annie, they hit me with a gun."

"Dear Lord."

Suddenly, I felt very weary. The anger and adrenalin that had kept me going since morning seemed to dribble out of me. We talked a couple minutes more.

"God, I hurt. Oh, God!"

"Didn't they give you something for the pain?"

"Yes. But it's not helping." But, in a few minutes, his eyes flickered and then stayed closed. The medicine was working.

I leaned over and kissed him on his relatively unbruised forehead. Even so, he winced a little.

In my car, I pulled out the list of accommodations given to me at the admittance desk and chose the nearest one. "Captain Josiah Jeffrey's Cozy Rest" proved to be a grand old Victorian house painted in mustard, rusty reds, and green, truly a painted lady.

Inside Mrs. Captain Jeffrey, a voluptuous white-haired matron dressed in ruffled purple greeted me with two out-stretched arms and a veritable gale of lavender scent. She so reminded me of "the Pooch" I started to call her "Letitia" when I thanked her for showing me her one remaining vacant room. It was tiny and overdressed. A whatnot stood in one corner. The brass bed was covered with a lavender duvet and almost a dozen pillows and shams of various shades of purple and pink. The tiny dressing table had a glass top and several variously shaped perfume bottles across the top leaving little room for a brush and comb. The one window had rich, velvet, deep purple drapes pooling onto the floor and a lavender lace valance across the front. I shared a tiny bathroom with the next room.

Locking the door to the next room, I stripped off my clothes and drew a nice hot bath taking advantage of some of the bubble bath the bed and breakfast provided. I sank in into the hot bubbles and soaked. When the water cooled, I dried myself with a huge towel and wrapped another around me. Then I washed out my underpants and spread them on the radiator to dry. I had no change of clothes. Tossing most of the pillows to the far side of the bed, I turned back the covers and slid into bed and was asleep in five minutes.

Chapter Nine

Silver light seeped through the blinds of my tiny window. Rolling over, I saw it was already seven. I sat up and ran my fingers through my hair. Water ran in my shared bathroom. Then it stopped, and a door opened and shut. My turn. I wrapped the bath towel around me, just in case. The bathroom was steamy from the other guest's shower. I showered and then brushed my teeth with my finger and hot water. Spotting some mouthwash, I gave my mouth a quick rinse, deciding not to notice whether it was provided by the bed and breakfast or belonged to the guest whose shaving gear was spread cross the vanity counter.

Dressing quickly, the waistband of my panties was still damp, I rummaged through my purse looking for lipstick and a comb. Finding none, I bit my lips until they were pink and not very successfully finger-combed my wavy hair. Not feeling at all confident of my appearance, I emerged from my room with some hesitation and came down the stairs wondering how many other guests would see me in Mrs. Jeffrey's dining room.

No other guests were eating. It wasn't until I was sipping Mrs. Jeffrey's wonderful coffee I began to consider my situation and my, or rather, *our*, itinerary for the day. I could expect to spend the morning, at least, waiting, for Steve's x-rays.

Mrs. Jeffrey plopped a huge plate of bacon, eggs, home fries, and toast in front of me. I remembered I had eaten nothing yesterday but a few tuna fish sandwiches. I polished off my breakfast leaving not a crumb and had more coffee. I still had no idea if Steve would be in the hospital another night or what, but I surely would like to buy a few toiletries for myself if he would be staying. At the very least, I wanted lipstick and a comb. I settled with Mrs. Jeffrey and told her I would call her on my cell phone as soon as I knew if I had to stay another night.

The big woman smiled and chuckled, her ample bosom jiggling with her laughter. She told me the location of a nearby CVS so I could pick up "a few things" as she put it. She had noticed I had arrived with no luggage.

Angels must've been watching over me. Because according to Mrs. Jeffrey, I was to drive west past the town green where I'd find a small shopping center. But, as I approached the green, I saw a tall steeple belonging to a congregational church, so newly painted white it glistened in the sun. A signboard announced the sermon would be: "Many would rejoice at his birth." Below it, a second sign announced the thrift shop was open on Saturdays and Mondays. Breaking hard, I squealed into the church parking lot. It was not until I got out of the car that I saw the store was open only from ten to eleven, and it was only about nine now. The angels were still smiling on me for before I could climb back into my car, a side door of the church swung open and a tall gray-haired lady wearing a clerical collar, a very tweedy skirt and rumpled cardigan came out.

"Er, good morning. Are you the pastor?"

"Good morning to you too. Yes, I'm Pastor Jean. Can I help you?"

I babbled my story as quickly as I could and hoped she would have perhaps some—ah—under things in her thrift shop.

She threw her head back and laughed merrily. "Oh, indeed, the Lord works in mysterious ways. Come in. Come in. Just yesterday, a member of my congregation brought these in and I thought, 'whoever in the world would want this package of undies?' Here, take them."

She didn't want money, so I looked around, browsing for maybe half an hour, then bought a royal blue turtleneck and a couple green plaid placemats and gave the good lady six bucks. I found the CVS, no problem, and picked up a toothbrush, comb, lipstick, and a couple of mags.

After parking in the hospital's visitor lot, I sat in the car for a while. I had thinking to do. When I realized it was close to lunchtime, I headed for the hospital's lunchroom. I figured they may not have results from the x-rays yet, so why sit with an irritable husband with whom I was so angry any longer than I had to. So, grabbing one of their grubby brown trays, I passed through the cafeteria line selecting a beef sandwich, an apple, big chocolate chip cookie, and coffee. It all looked either dried up, withered, or just institutional. I was right. The coffee was dishwater, the apple, brown, and soft in places, and the sandwich tasteless. I lingered as long as I reasonably could and then went upstairs to see Steve and deal with whatever had to be dealt with.

As I approached Steve's ward, I saw a tall man in a blue uniform outside the ward entrance. He was a member of the local police force. He held out his arm to block my entrance. After identifying myself, he informed me my husband, upon his release, would be escorted to Massachusetts. I was speechless. What was happening? My eyes filled with tears as I scurried in to see Steve.

Steve's bed was empty. I pulled up the straight-backed chair and settled down to wait. I had pretty much thumbed through my magazines when I heard the squeaking wheels of a gurney coming down the corridor. I hurried out into the hallway and Steve lifted a hand in greeting and attempted a smile on the less bruised side of his face. But he looked ashen and his bruises had deepened into red and purple welts. Once they had him settled, I took my chair again.

"Got tree teef shwining," attempted my husband, pointing to his mouth and the teeth he wobbled back and forth with his tongue.

"We'll see a dentist as soon as we get home," I said and immediately wondered how we'd pay for it. We had no dental insurance. "What did the x-rays show?"

"Don know. Way for doctor."

"Well, nothing to do but wait."

I got up and walked to the ward window to stretch my legs and ease my stiff back. Really just for something to do. The window provided a beautiful view of the brick wing of the newer part of the hospital. When the doctor arrived an hour later, his manner was somewhat changed from last night. He was stiff and curt, seemingly uncomfortable and wanting to get done with his job. I think the policeman outside the door had something to do with it. I saw him speak briefly with the doctor.

"Basically, your husband has three broken ribs and three teeth knocked very loose, as well as contusions on his face, arms, and chest, and even the abdomen. We have done what we could." The doctor handed me a printed sheet with instructions for the care of cracked ribs, and before I could do more than glance at it, he handed me a slip of paper—a prescription for pain reliever. Quickly, I put both in my purse. "Normally, I would advise you to see his primary immediately upon returning home, but under the circumstances..." Something at the doorway caught his attention and he stopped mid-sentence.

What followed was something of a blur. The doctor got no further in his instructions when Pereira and

Roderiques came barging through the doorway. At the sight of those two, my stomach lurched. Talk about a gut reaction. That horrible lunch felt like a rock in my gut.

Someone said, "Get him dressed."

Steve screamed as I tried to sit him up and put a shirt on him.

The orderly appeared. "Let me help with that." God bless him, he ever so gently got Steve into his clothes while I sat on the little chair both frightened and angry.

I heard Pereira saying how hospital checks made it easy and something about finding the Cherokee with a gun in the glove compartment. Steve yelled he owned no gun.

Roderiques snorted. "You sure don't. It wasn't registered. You know what that means." When I heard: "You have the right to remain silent. Do you understand what this means?"

I jumped up and ran to Steve thinking: *But this is real life not some stupid cop show on TV.*

A burley officer in blue stepped between me and my husband and I heard the clatter of handcuffs. Steve was hustled into a wheelchair and rolled into the corridor.

The motorcycle accident kid called out, "Oh, wow! Cool, man! So long, buddy!" as the doctor took Pereira by the sleeve and whispered a few words to him.

I heard Pereira respond, "Don't worry. Ash Street has a decent infirmary."

I followed them out.

Roderiques came and said, "I'll drive you home, Mrs. Rendle."

Sitting in the front seat and staring at the light rain spattering the windshield, I asked, rather idiotically, "Is he arrested? Will he go to jail?"

Roderiques sort of grimaced and grunted. I wasn't sure if that was a yes or no. A car pulled into our lane in front of us and slowed. Roderiques tapped his brakes, my brakes, and swore. I glanced at him. His jaw was clenched, and he looked grim. I wasn't going to ask *him* anything.

The drive to New Bedford seemed to last forever with the traffic getting ever heavier. For the most part, neither of us said a word. But my thoughts were swirling, trying to make sense of it all. Why was Steve being arrested when, I would have thought, the guys who beat him up should be the ones wearing the handcuffs.

Finally, I simply had to ask, "Why was Steve arrested when it was Ramona's gang that beat him up?"

"You're way out in left field, Mrs. Rendle." His eyes slid for a moment from the road to my face. Seeing my total incomprehension, he sighed and said, "Now don't go all hysterical female on me. It's just we got some evidence he may be involved in that arson case—the lawyer's office."

"Oh—my God," I said softly clutching my arms across my chest as if trying physically to keep myself from going "all hysterical female" on Roderiques. Then, finally, sucking in a deep breath and letting it out again in a gust. "Oh. My God in Heaven."

"You know something about that, do you?" It was more a statement than a question.

"No! Yes, no! I don't know."

He waited me out.

"He was my Aunt Sarah's lawyer. The only copy of her will was in that office. That's what I know." I decided I wouldn't say anything about the invalid will we found in my aunt's house. Somehow, I was suddenly afraid the cops would think I was breaking and entering her house. I needed time to think about that. I needed time to think about a lot of things. That Steve had been involved in anything so horrible as arson was unbelievable—yet there was that jacket.

Deciding that being silent would suit Roderiques and was, yes, safer for me, I said nothing more for the rest of the ride. But I kept turning things over in my mind. Had Steve really done this thing? No, that was not my Steve. I could not really believe my scholarly, sedentary professor husband would take such an active role in anything. His reaction to his gambling problems had been to flee. But he if *had* done this, then he must somehow be involved in the distribution of my aunt's estate and, oh my God, the police may be thinking he murdered Aunt Sarah.

Yeah. They would think that. That was their business. I blotted my eyes several times with a tissue, blew my nose, but said nothing to the police officer driving my car.

"Steve is no murderer," I blurted as we pulled onto Union Street.

"No one said he was."

But when we drove past that huge brick, windowless, rambling building standing taller than the neighboring homes, its rolls of barbed wire along the roof line glinting in the fading light—the Ash Street Jail—I could hold it in no longer. Try as I would, my eyes welled with tears and I fumbled for more tissues.

"Now, now, Mrs. Rendle, you've been doing great. You've been really brave. You are almost home." His voice was surprisingly soft.

Few more twists and turns and we were there. As we pulled into my driveway, I saw a police cruiser waiting in front of my house, for Roderiques, I assumed. It was only then I remembered I had intended to tell detective Pereira about the missing violets.

"I'd been taking care of my aunt's violets. When I went to water them the last time they were gone."

"All of them?"

"No. Sorry. The hybrids she was so proud of and wanted to sell commercially. They were gone."

"You are sure?"

"Positive. I searched all over for them." I started to get out of my car. I had one foot out the door when Roderiques took my arm. "Wait a minute, Mrs. Rendle." He held onto me despite my protests that I wasn't going anywhere, and he made a call to Pereira, I presumed.

"He wants to talk to you tomorrow morning, okay?"

I nodded and whimpered I'd like my car keys.

"Oh, sorry." He turned off the engine and pulled out my keys. It was amazing the possession of one's own keys could do.

I felt much empowered. The tears dried up as I climbed out of my set of wheels and banged the door shut. Roderiques followed immediately and strode off to the waiting cruiser. I beeped the car locked.

As I was opening my front door, I noticed an old VW square-back crawl by. It was dark green with one blue front fender. It almost stopped, but then, as if seeing the police cruiser there, it picked up a little speed and went by.

Locking myself in, I stood looking out the front window until the police car left. It took its sweet time, but, in reality, had sat there only a minute. I took a deep breath and tried to shrug the tension out of my shoulders. Despite everything, it was good to be home.

"Mrrt!" Rollo sprang to the arm of the easy chair purring and kneading the upholstery. Hearing his claws pricking and clawing at the material sounded so homey and familiar, I had no heart to scold him. "You must be so hungry." Then with a little chirrup he leaped at me and landed on my shoulder. "Oh, my kitty, my kitty, it is so good to see you." It was so comforting to see him I did not pull him from my shoulder, but with my hand stretched around to his back and with him still tottering on my shoulder, we walked together into the kitchen.

"Rollo! Yuck!" Spread across the floor was Rollo's culinary collection. My overnight absence and his Yankee ingenuity had resulted in a display of two pairs of bird legs and one large "emptied" mouse. Rollo jumped from my shoulder and stood before his empty water dish. The big cat stared up at me and meowed so piteously I rushed to fill his water bowl before I cleaned up the mess on my floor. "Thirsty work catching your own meals, huh, fella." But his food dish was not anywhere near empty. Hmm. Looked like he had an opinion on what he preferred to eat. I tried to remember what flavor of Yummy Feast I had put down for him. I would not buy that kind again. No use. I could not remember which kind it was, and I was not going to pick through the garbage for the empty can. I got out the broom and dustpan and set to work cleaning up the kitchen floor.

Once I had the disgusting stuff cleaned away and a fresh bowl of salmon feast put down for him, which he accepted, settling down to nibble delicately, I realized how hungry I was. That soft apple and dry sandwich eaten in the hospital were ancient history. I stared into the refrigerator. Hunger and exhaustion fought with one another. Cooking seemed like a big hurdle. I pulled out some lettuce and celery. I hadn't eaten fresh veggies for two days. A salad seemed good and succulent, but a lot of work to prepare. Celery sticks would have to do.

I might find some burgers in the freezer. I was so tired dragging out the skillet seemed like heavy work. That was when the microwave was such a blessing. I was setting frozen burgers on a plate to microwave when I heard footsteps on the porch.

The doorbell buzzed. Now who could that be? Certainly not Steve. One of Gerry's enforcers? Dear God, I hoped not. The bell buzzed again. *Guess I had better answer it.* I slipped the chain on the door and opened it the few inches the chain allowed. I was nose-to-nose with Joe Brown's floppy mug.

"Joe!" I swung the door open wide. "What brings you here?"

"Wanna go for a spin?" said my ex-con chum, gesturing toward the road. "Where ya been, anyway? I was by a couple times yesterday and you wasn't here."

"Long story." Out by the curb stood an ancient VW square-back dark green with one navy blue front fender. "Hey, were you here when the cops dropped me off? Seems there was a square-back across the street when I got home."

"Yeah, but I didn't want to get anywhere near any cops."

"Joe, have you had any supper yet?"

"No, but it's not yet five."

"I'm starved. Let's go for a spin to Tony's, my treat."

"Okay, but I'm not real hungry, but since you are treatin', I'll manage a slice or two," he grinned.

I stepped back inside and grabbed my jacket and purse. I knew Joe had been saving every penny he could hold onto to get a set of wheels, and that old VW was like a Lexus for him. I climbed into the passenger seat ignoring the torn upholstery and puffy white stuff peeking through the rip in the seat and we putt-putted and rattle-rattled away.

Tony's World's Best Pizza was in Dartmouth on Route 6 near the mall. At this hour it was still pretty much deserted, but soon folks would be stopping in for their Saturday night pizza to go with their Sam Adams and rented or downloaded movie. Tony's was a cozy family-oriented place. One ordered from a pass-through counter where two high school girls worked at a furious pace taking orders, making up subs, salads, and pouring beverages while behind them Tony made the pizza. Mostly it was take-out, but there were Formica-topped tables with a spatter pattern of tiny gold stars imprinted in the surface. The artist in me always wondered—and I did even this evening—

what an artist was paid for coming up with such an insipid design. Every table was set with a skinny milk glass vase holding three fake chrysanthemums, napkins, salt, pepper, a jar of hot pepper flakes, and patrons were expected to bus their own tables. We found a small table in the farthest corner; what I had to tell Joe was not for general neighborhood distribution. Since I was paying and was ravenous, we went for a large pizza supreme everything on it, salads, coffee, and later maybe we would finish off with ice cream, or so my growling stomach told me. I told Joe everything about my and Steve's horrendous experiences. He listened, munching on his pizza and nodding silently.

"He'll be arraigned on Monday. I'm not exactly sure for what."

"A good guess would for that handgun and for burning down the lawyer's office."

"Steve would never do that." Much as I was angry with my husband, I still sort of automatically defended Steve. I could not believe what was becoming more evident. This was not like the kind of real life I knew about. This was TV.

"The jacket," Joe said softly.

I sat back in my chair and blinked back tears. Yeah, the jacket; that would not go away. Once again, I thought of its stomach-churning gasoline smell.

"Listen, Anna, whoever burned that building down may have wanted your aunt's will destroyed. She probably left everything to her kids. That would be normal. Could be the fake will was planted by the same someone, let's say Steve, hoping you would inherit a lot of cash, and, as his wife, help him out of his money problems. That may be an ugly scenario, but it fits the evidence, you are gonna have to face up to it. I know I'm being blunt, but, heck, the reality is the man's in jail."

Oh my God! The tears ran down my face. I turned to the wall and dried my eyes with paper napkins as two men and a woman came into the store, one holding a Redbox envelope.

"Here, switch seats with me." I wanted to sit with my back to the stream of customers that had started coming in. I didn't want them to see me weepy. I dabbed my eyes and blew my nose. I stared right into Joe's sad, puppy dog eyes and then looked down. I picked up a last piece of pizza and nibbled the crust. Chewing would give me a moment to try to reason things through. Had Steve lost his sanity altogether or was he so desperate he could burn down a building, possibly killing someone inside? I did not think him insane when I took him to the hospital. At the time, I thought of him as a weak man in terrible pain. And, if not insane, what motive could he have had other than to destroy Aunt Sarah's will? Then I recalled how encouraging he was of Joe and me going into her house and finding the second will. Had he wanted us to find it? Good grief! Had he planted it there? If yes, and I had to think the answer was yes, then the big question: Did he get this idea after my aunt's death or did he, dear God, kill her?

At this thought, I looked up sharply at Joe. He nodded.

"Did he kill her, Joe?"

"No doubt that's what the police think."

I sat still for several moments. All the events of the last two weeks raced through my brain. Maybe it was Joe's friendly presence, or the warm strengthening meal, or maybe I really did have the backbone, but then and there I resolved not to defend Steve anymore.

"Okay, where do we go from here?"

Not really hearing Joe's questioning, "We?" I jumped up.

"I want my pistachio ice cream."

Joe laughed so loudly all the patrons in the place looked up, as I ran up to the pass-through counter.

"Make that two."

As we scraped the last of the sweet green liquid from our bowls, Joe asked, "You told Roderiques about the violets, right? Do the cops know about the fake will?"

"Not unless Mr. Jepson told them."

"Tell them."

Chapter Ten

I couldn't sleep most of the night. Finally, in the early morning hours, I dropped into turbulent, restless sleep, with one nightmare after another—Steve was sentenced, then executed by Gatling gun, then he was hanged, and after that, guillotined.

I woke up around 7:30. Rollo was demanding food, walking up and down on Steve's side of the bed. When I did not rouse myself soon enough to please him, he stepped on my stomach, sat on my belly, and kicked himself, scratching his ear with his hind leg. Ooph! He weighed a ton. I shoved him off and rolled out of bed. Not until my feet hit the cold floor did the fog of my nightmares dissipate and my brain rejoin the real world. Steve was very much alive. In fact, it would be a dreary day of waiting, of filling in the hours until Monday came when Steve would be arraigned. I had no idea what to expect and dreaded Monday immensely.

I shuffled into the bathroom and, after donning my bathrobe and slippers, went downstairs to the kitchen. There, Rollo polished my calves and I quickly opened a can of his favorite food. I started the coffee and went out the front door, still in my robe, for the paper. I was trying hard not to think of Steve, or our, future. But I did think. I thought of *my* future. Maybe I really was ready, after my resolution of last evening, to put Steve on the backburner of my life. Whatever that meant.

I paged listlessly through the newspaper glancing at the want ads. Why? I didn't know. I wasn't looking for employment, not now, at least. I guessed I wanted to see what was there. What I would do if I needed to find a job. There were so few ads in the employment section in this computer age. There was football news *ad nauseum*. I thought the paper recorded every tactic the Patriots used against their opponents. I was not a big fan, but I tried to read some of it to take my mind off my own problems. It didn't work. I could not concentrate on anyone else's business.

While slowly chewing on toast I found hard to swallow and spooning in a little cold cereal, I was pleased, at least, to find no mention of my aunt's murder nor of the arson on the local news pages. Just as I finished eating, the clouds hanging over New Bedford parted, and sunshine streamed into the kitchen lighting up the table where I sat and casting a yellow patch of sunshine over the floor and the cat food dishes where Rollo sat washing his face. As the room filled with bright, optimistic light, I felt a little more capable and hopeful. I dressed and decided I needed to see people.

I still had time to make the service at Aunt Sarah's church. It might do me some good, and then I would attend to her violets, as I knew they would want watering again, and then, finally, I'd try to reach the police about the second will. It seemed like a good plan for the day.

As I pulled into the church parking lot, little kids clutching Sunday school leaflets and some sort of craft project were skittering in many directions like leaves blown by the wind, their mothers and fathers hurrying to take hold of little hands and get them safely into cars. The family service was over. In a few minutes, the parking lot pandemonium would be over and the more formal eleven o'clock service would begin. I waited, and when the little ones were on their way home, I found a parking spot where I would not have to back up to get out. I did not want to hit one of the little cherubs or some bent over old lady of which there seemed to be a fair number.

Locking the car door, I stood for a moment straightening my jacket and taking a deep breath. This was Aunt Sarah's church, and though I had gone with her a number of times I was not a member. Going in, I stepped first into the ladies' room to straighten my hair. Sonya Gundersen was standing by the sink. When she turned and saw me, her expression was anything but pleasant, more like dried prunes.

I almost backed out of the room but took a deep breath and forced myself to wish her a cheery, "Good morning, Sonya." I did not know her well, but I knew she was one of my aunt's friends, whether from the sewing circle or the African violet club, I wasn't sure.

She gave a short nod. "You're Sarah's niece, aren't you? She was getting prideful—about her violets. Maybe she was judged."

Wow! That was certainly unexpected. I brushed past her without saying a word and went into one of the stalls where I stayed until she left the bathroom and I had recovered from her rude remark.

Marta was a greeter and her eyes grew huge with surprise and something else as she handed me the bulletin. I slipped into the very last pew feeling like a stranger. The choir anthem was beautiful, the children's sermon, funny. Everyone laughed. And the sermon was all about the Lord's love based on St. Paul's epistles. I did feel better as I left, especially since the pastor remembered me and offered his condolences. Several others offered kind words and hugs, although Marta gave me a weird look and started to say something, but thought better of it, when someone tapped softly on my arm.

I turned and was looking into the gentle gray eyes of Priscilla Bronstad. Shyly, she tried to tell me they had a women's group here—a sewing circle—and they did a lot of good for others and for each other. When she got to the words "each other", she patted my arm meaningfully and looked at the floor.

I gave Aunt Sarah's bashful friend a little hug and whispered, "Thank you." She had made me feel so welcome.

Going home, I saw the trees were at their bright October peak of color. Brilliant golds, salmons, yellows, and pinks decorated the branches. Only the oaks were holding back, sticking to dull, bronzy green. The Sunday world looked beautiful and life seemed possible again.

Home again, I changed into jeans and an old sweatshirt and, after giving Rollo a treat, I scratched his ears for ten minutes. This was a ploy on my part. I had noticed a long ear rub calmed him into taking a nap and perhaps, I hoped, would discourage him from bringing something nasty into my kitchen while I was gone.

I drove to Aunt Sarah's house. As I approached the driveway, I thought I saw something move near my aunt's garage, a small dog perhaps, running toward her watchful neighbor's house. Couldn't be the old woman because when I pulled fully into the driveway, I saw the curtain flick and knew the old neighbor lady glimpsed at me. I waved and smiled at her. Ah, well, if there was anything wrong, she'd have let me know, bless her heart.

Muddy footprints led up the steps to the back-porch door. Someone had been here since yesterday's rain! But who? I carefully avoided stepping into the muddy prints; they were something else I would now have to tell the police. I had left the screen door unlatched. I knew that, but when I went to unlock the back door, it swung open at my touch. It had not been locked or even pulled firmly shut. I froze. A shiver ran down my spine. Was someone inside my aunt's house? Should I ask Mrs. Tripp next door? No, best not to frighten the poor old thing.

Trying to act like everything was perfectly normal I walked slowly back to my car and got in. Then I thought of Joe. Had he come to his old friend and mentor's house? Had he perhaps remembered something of his he had left there? It was not likely, I thought. And those prints did not seem big enough to have been made by his big old boots. If he was working at Shay's today, he'd be about done by now. Instinctively, I pulled out my cell phone to call him. Then I remembered he had no telephone. Joe had sunk all his meager wages into his old VW. I backed out of the driveway. If I hurried, I might catch him at Shay's or maybe at his apartment.

"Please, God, make him be where I can get hold of him," I muttered through gritted teeth as I put the car into drive and roared down the street.

Three minutes later, I pulled into the employees' lot behind Shay's. I was in luck for I immediately spotted Joe's old VW with its mismatched fenders. I drew up beside it. Slamming my car door shut, I went streaking toward the market, beeping my car locked as I reached the loading platform. The great door was rolled down and the regular door for human entrance was also closed.

But a high schooler was sweeping up lettuce leaves next to a stack of empty wooden crates. I climbed up the steps to the loading dock. The boy stopped his sweeping and stared, picking at his acne. He didn't seem to know what he should do with me, a strange lady coming to the back of the store. He started to say, "You gotta go around..."

I asked him if Joe Brown was still here.

He leaned the broom against the wall and stuck his head in the door yelling, "Hey, Joe! Your wife is here!"

A much-surprised Joe peeked out the door, laughed, then grinned. "Just a minute, honey, while I punch out." A few seconds later, Joe appeared in the doorway slipping on his jacket. "Okay, sweetheart, let's get going." He gave me a quick spousal peck on the lips.

Despite myself, I had to laugh. "You're a pretty good actor," I said.

"Well, you told that kid."

"I didn't. He just assumed."

Joe threw his head back and roared.

"Joe, this is serious. I'm frightened," I explained as we rode in my car back to Aunt Sarah's house.

Before we got out of the car, Joe opened my glove compartment and poked around inside.

"What are you doing?'

"Lookin' for a weapon."

"Whaaat?" I yelled. Visions of the gun the police found in Steve's car played through my head.

Joe slammed the glove compartment door shut and began feeling around under the front seat. "Ah. Here we go." Joe pulled the heavy black flashlight Steve had put under the seat for emergencies.

"That's been there a long time," I said. "The batteries are probably dead."

"Doesn't matter. Just want a little protection." Holding the bulb end of the flashlight, Joe gave it a firm whack against the palm of his right hand. Satisfied it would give a solid blow, he opened his door. "Okay. Let's go."

When we reached my aunt's back door, it was locked. I hadn't locked it.

"Good thing you didn't go in. Someone hadn't finished what he was doing." Joe's whisper sounded like gravel in his throat.

Joe went in first. I stayed right behind him, sort of hiding behind his bulk. I was that disturbed. No one was in the kitchen, but it seemed, different, wrong somehow, abnormally quiet. Slowly, we moved from room to room on the first floor. No one was there, and nothing seemed disturbed. Joe turned suddenly and went back to the kitchen. He returned clutching a small iron skillet in one of his big paws and handed me the flashlight.

"Just in case," he whispered.

Thus armed, we started slowly up the stairs. We crept down the hallway, with Joe testing floorboards for noisy creaks with tentative toe taps. We went from room to room, gently pushing open doors, and looking into every nook and cranny. No one was there, and nothing seemed out of place. Lastly, we entered my aunt's bedroom where she had been killed. I had not wanted to go in that room again.

"Holy..." rumbled Joe, a stream of gutter words followed. He pushed me back with his arm. "Maybe you better not go in, Annie."

But I already had peered around his shoulder. "Oh!" I squeaked, all I could add to Joe's string of expletives.

The room had been torn apart. The mattress had been stabbed in several places and stuffing puffed through the slashes. Giant circles were scrawled over the wallpaper. "I'm back" was written on the dressing table mirror in flaming red lipstick. The little drawers of the dressing table were pulled out and their contents spilled out on the floor. Clothing lay strewn on the floor. Worst of all, in my opinion, the painting of Uncle Matthias that hung by the window was torn so that a large flap of what had been his face hung down and written on its back in pencil was, "Take that, you, old, violet-pissing bird!"

Tears burst from my eyes and I pawed at them with both fists. "She loved that picture. It was an oil painting," I said rather pointlessly.

Joe took my elbow. "Let's go back downstairs."

We went into the kitchen and sat down at the kitchen table. Joe waited me out while I cried like there was no tomorrow.

When I could cry no more, I looked up at Joe.

"You've got a lot to tell the cops."

"Uh-huh."

Joe didn't move. He continued to look into my eyes. I reached into my purse. "Maybe I should call them now."

"Yeah."

I punched in Pereira's number. Directed to leave a message, I mumbled a few words and left my number. I didn't know where to begin. "Guess he has Sundays off."

"No. There was a stabbin'. Didn't you see it on the news?"

"I didn't see the news."

"No, I guess not. You was bein' a good little girl. Sittin' in church." The slightest ghost of a smile dimpled Joe's cheeks. "Three guys in the South End."

"Oh, dear. How awful," I said without much feeling. I wasn't capable of feeling anything for three guys in the South End, West End, or any other end.

"Yeah, I saw about it on my break on the TV in the employees' room. One dead, one nearly gone, and the other critical."

We sat quietly for several minutes. I thought again about how weirdly quiet the kitchen seemed. The clock was not ticking. I straightened and looked over my shoulder. It was gone! How long had it been missing? My aunt had a Felix the Cat clock given to her by an old friend. It was so silly looking she said she could only hide it in the kitchen. It was black with a comic smile and big white eyes with green pupils that rolled back and forth as its pendulum tail kept time. How could I have not noticed it was gone? One more thing to mention to Pereira. Had it been taken today? When the bedroom was ripped apart?

Joe's stomach growled, and he looked at his watch.

"You haven't had lunch either, have you?" I asked.

He shook his head.

I stood. "I must water the violets. I'll try to be quick about it. Then we'll eat."

I went into the violet room, put on one of my aunt's canvas aprons, and filled a watering can. Everything looked all right in the little plant room. Methodically, I watered the trays in which the plants sat, being very careful not to wet the violet leaves. I was halfway down the right-hand side of the room when I noticed a plant's label had a red violet pictured on it. The trouble was, it was a beautiful plant bursting with white blooms. I pulled out the tag and looked closely at it. Obviously, it was meant for a different variety. Not knowing where to put it, I stuck it back into the white-flowered plant. The next plant had orange flowers, but its tag showed it as a white variety. I went up and down the rows of plants. Not all, but several more labels were obviously misplaced. For all I knew, all of them may have been switched because I was not familiar enough with all the subtle shades of violet, purple, and fuchsia.

"Joe, our house invader is not only vicious and violent, but also mischievous."

"More to tell the cops about."

I refilled the watering can and finished giving the violets their drink. "Let's get out of here. This dear old house is giving me the creeps." Then quickly, before leaving, I ran back upstairs. I lifted the torn oil painting off the wall and came back into the kitchen with it.

"I'm going to see if I can have this restored. I'll call Cookie about it. It is hers after all, but I bet she'll agree. I have to call her anyway about changing the locks."

"The sooner, the better," rumbled Joe.

"Yeah, but I can't be acting like this was my place."

As soon as I thought of the house being Cookie's property, I felt a twinge in my heart. Down deep, I realized I wished it was my place. How sad it would be to have Cookie in possession of the old house. She'd probably sell it.

After locking and checking all the doors, I drove back to Shay's so Joe could get his car and I dashed inside to pick up a few things for a late lunch and supper. Joe followed me home. I had promised him a pastrami sandwich.

As we came into the kitchen, there was no sign of Rollo, but in the very center of the kitchen floor was a mouse and the largest eviscerated blue jay I had ever seen. The bird was laying spread-eagled. A few wing feathers had drifted into Rollo's water dish.

"Joe, have seat in the living room while I clean up Rollo's presents," I called over my shoulder, setting down my groceries on the kitchen table. "Oh, that cat!"

Just as I said that, I felt his furry flanks rubbing against the backs of my calves and hear his loud purring as I tossed the mouse into the garbage by its tail. "Oh, Rollo! Yes, I do love you, but did you have to choose this moment to gift us with dead creatures?"

I got out the broom and dust pan and made quick work of the remainder of Rollo's offerings. Then set to work making pastrami sandwiches. I called in Joe and spilled out some potato chips onto our plates. I made myself tea. Joe settled for water. We ate. I was famished. I was eager to try to get a hold of Cookie and Pereira. We talked a little about the arraignment tomorrow. Joe said he had Monday off, so he would come to the courthouse in case he could be of any help. He was, he reminded me, familiar, unfortunately, with the arraignment process.

After his old VW put-putted out of sight, I sat in the living room to put my feet up and center myself. I finished my mug of tea, leaning back against the quilt on the sofa. It made a soft crunching sound like that of crinkled paper. My head was swirling with thoughts about criminal case lawyers, bail bondsmen, and I paid no attention to my aunt's quilt. What would I need to do for Steve?

After a while, I went to my phone intending to call Cookie or at least leave a message for her. I wasn't sure if the number I had for her was her home phone, cell, or business. When I got to my phone, my answering machine was blinking. Pereira and Roderiques were coming this afternoon to see me at four o'clock. It was past three now. I scrambled to make myself presentable, comb my hair, put on fresh lipstick. Neatened up, I found myself pacing the living room, waiting.

It seemed like they were here for hours. There was so much to tell and so many questions from the invalid will, the stolen hybrids, the footprints, stolen clock, and ransacked house, to the mislabeled plants. They immediately called for someone to look at the footprints, because rain was promised for tonight, and a return call claimed they were most likely from a woman's boots. They sent pictures on their cell phones. I was grilled. They seemed to think I had unwittingly made the footprints myself. I wasn't that dumb I protested. Besides, it was only October; I hadn't worn boots yet. Nevertheless, they insisted on seeing all my shoes, saying they needed to be thorough, and it was routine.

They looked at every pair of shoes I owned. First, we looked inthe front hall closet where our snow boots etc. were kept. Then I led them upstairs to my bedroom closet. I wanted to make sure they didn't peek anywhere else but that closet. My shoes were stuffed into a twelve-pocket bag that hung on the back of my closet door. It didn't take them more than a quick glance to see my shoes could never have made those prints. However, Roderiques couldn't contain himself. He pulled out a dainty, metallic silvery high heeled sandal, one of the pairs I'd worn at my wedding, and made a crack to the effect he felt like the prince with the glass slipper.

To his credit, Pereira immediately snapped, "That's why you're a sergeant and probably will never be a detective."

It was well past dinnertime when they left. Pereira said he would talk to Cookie first, then let me know when I could call her about changing the locks. I started to protest, I wanted to call her and get it done quickly.

He scowled and said, "Let me remind you, ma'am, we may still have a murderer on the loose," and then mumbled something about proper procedure as they went out the door.

I was opening cans for mine and Rollo's supper. I didn't have much appetite, but the cat certainly did. My feline companion stretched full length against the kitchen cabinet and let out a piteous yowl, informing me he had not been fed in weeks. "Liar," I said as I set down his dish of fancy food and stroked his back.

That was when it dawned on me. Pereira had said they may still have a murderer on the loose. *May.* They *were* still thinking Steve may be the killer. Until now, I hadn't really believed they were thinking my husband involved in anything worse than leaving the state and having an unregistered gun. I realized I may have reinforced their belief in his guilt by telling them about the fake will that had made me an heiress and by implication resolved all Steve's money problems. Mrs. Tripp's evidence placing a man of Steve's description outside my aunt's house didn't help. Then with the direct evidence of his jacket found, I supposed, at the arson site and its possible connection through the loss of my aunt's will to the murder case, they would be thinking they had a strong case against him.

Oh, Steve! What had I done? You could never harm anybody! They didn't know you like I did.

Rollo leapt up onto the table and stood in front of me right over my empty plate he purred loudly and head-bumped my chin. Offering himself for petting.

"Rollo, good boy. You are trying to comfort me, aren't you? Good, good kitty." I scratched his chin.

The phone rang. It was Pereira. He gave the okay for me to call Cookie, and even supplied her cell phone number. After that, he was not willing to say much about the case except they were pursuing every path.

Every path? Maybe they were not completely convinced Steve was the murderer. I was perhaps grasping at a straw, but wow! I could feel the tension slipping off my shoulders like an out-going tide. I jumped up and put the kettle on. When I had myself settled with a nice cup of Red Rose, I punched in Cookie's number.

"Yeah? Oh, it's you. I thought it might be. I just got done with the cops." Cookie sounded both angry and frightened. "I don't know what you've been telling them but—"

I interrupted her before she could get up a good head of steam. I explained I hadn't said anything to the police about her, but we had some real issues about the house. Quickly, I filled her in about all the vandalism and theft. She agreed without a moment's pause to the lock change and gave me her address to mail the new keys. As to the painting, she said she did not remember it and I could have it as far as she was concerned. I said I'd try to have it restored and the heirs could then do as they liked.

At this point, I had no idea when things would be settled, and she could clean out her mother's things. The house was still a crime scene, I thought, especially after this last instance of vandalism.

She ended by saying she wished the whole thing would soon be over and hung up without a word of sympathy for me about Steve. Strange she did not express curiosity as to who would steal her mother's plants. She had mentioned at the beginning of our conversation before I told her about the stolen violets she had been back East on business and just returned home. Then, after I had filled her in, she got very curt and was rather incurious, or so I thought, about the goings on at Aunt Sarah's house. Had she been there? Did she know more than she was letting on and didn't want to talk for fear of giving herself away? Could she possibly be...? Hmm. The footprints were of a woman's boots, the police said.

I sat a long while thinking things over. Much relieved the cops did not think my husband was a murderer, I started to nod off. Grandfather bonged, and I realized it was getting late. Slowly, Rollo and I climbed the stairs and headed for bed. I was exhausted but doubted I'd sleep much. Tomorrow was Steve's day in court.

Chapter Eleven

Joe took my elbow as we came down the courthouse steps. The arraignment was a horrible experience. Steve was handcuffed and shackled. At the end, I had reached out to him and was able to touch the sleeve of his shirt as they led him away. He turned and looked at me with the biggest, saddest eyes.

A lump the size of an apple rose in my throat. *That's my husband they are taking away*, I thought, seeing him in my mind the time we first met and fell in love. Immediately, I thought, *That's my husband, the man who so deceived me and whom I am thinking of leaving forever.*

As the door at the far end of the room closed behind him, I thought, *Now he's gone. It is over.* Not really, but it felt that way. I had no control. I could do nothing for him now. The judge had refused to grant him bail. Joe and I stood in the courtroom with me still leaning on the bar as everyone else cleared out.

Finally, a man in uniform, possibly a bailiff, gently touched my arm. "Ma'am, it is time for you to step outside." He and Joe walked me out of the courtroom and down the many steps, Joe taking my elbow, steering me with the gentlest pressure.

We were standing on the sidewalk when tears came. Joe put his arm around my shoulders and mumbled, "Now, now. You'll get through this."

A cold bitter wind blew up from the harbor and we walked into the teeth of it as we hurried down William Street to the Elm Street garage. Seagulls circled overhead, screeching. As we reached my car and I beeped the door unlocked. I whispered to Joe, "Thanks for being here for me," and stretched up on tiptoe and gave him a quick peck on the cheek.

Immediately, embarrassed, we both muttered something like, "See you soon," and I dove into my car. What was I thinking? I had kissed an ex-con. But he was not an ex-con to me, but a good friend. Probably my best friend these days. But I could still feel the stubble on his cheek and smell the scent of his skin as I drove onto Union Street and headed home.

On impulse, I pulled my car into a rare parking space, fed the meter, and entered the little coffee shop on the corner of Purchase and Union before going home. I didn't want to go to an empty house yet. It felt good having people milling around me in the shop. But I wanted time to think without having to talk to anyone.

Sitting by the window, I watched the passersby as I sipped a hot latte. I thought a little about Joe, what a good friend he'd been to me, that peck of a kiss, and then long about Steve. I replayed the whole courtroom scene in my mind, saw his frizzy-haired public defender lawyer and the Asian judge and shuddered at the upcoming trial. But I was dry-eyed.

I people watched. The folks outside on the street seemed a down-and-out crew. Of course, I realized the more fortunate had jobs and were in their offices at this hour. These were the folks heading for the soup kitchen in the next block. Then a person in a motorized wheelchair rolled by. I think she was woman, but it was hard to tell. She was so obese. A blubbery bosom avalanched over her knees, covering them. She looked like a mountain of adipose tissue poured into the wheelchair. I did not think a human being could get that large. She rolled by like she owned the sidewalk. Other people stepped aside. Looking at her made me realize, despite my troubles, I still had many blessings. If she could manage to cope in this old world, and with even a certain presumption, I could manage to handle what life's thrown my way.

I drained my cup, feeling more powerful than I had in days, and drove home.

When I got home, Rollo demanded chow and, of course, got it, even before I took off my jacket. I watched him chew for a minute, a furry oval with a tail stretched out behind him. I set the kettle on and made myself a sandwich.

After eating the sandwich, and still feeling the jolt of the latte, I settled on the couch with a mug of decaf tea. The house seemed cold, empty. What was I supposed to do now? I tried to sort through my options. How would I live without Steve's salary, if he was convicted of something? Of course, I would continue to draw and make my postcards, but they brought in only pin money, and paid my groceries at best. I vowed to start drawing tomorrow first thing in the morning. Perhaps, I should try teaching again somewhere, somehow, letting my bad back be a bad back and putting up with it. Immediately, I knew a classroom of even at the most angelic of kids would not work. I hated the idea of it. Then I considered maybe I could go back to that giftshop and turn out whale-tail T-shirts again, at least temporarily, assuming they needed help in this economy, which they probably didn't.

Sighing, I leaned back and heard the quilt crunch and once again I heard Aunt Sarah's voice or thought I did. "The quilt, Anna, the quilt."

Okay, so this time I'd take a close look at this quilt. I'd nothing else to do now anyway. Getting up, I spread out the quilt across the back and seat of the couch. Feeling with my hands, I determined that along one edge, a ten-inch or so strip with something crackly inside ran all along the length of the quilt. I could see nothing in the stitching that would give me any hint as to how this occurred. The compass rose pattern was intact and there was not a difference in color or stitching that I could see. I flipped the quilt over. Its backside was of a solid tan color, the color of old muslin. All of it. It was a tied quilt. I smoothed my hands over it. Did I feel a seam? The afternoon light was fading. I got up and went around the living room turning on every light in the room. Starting at the top of my aunt's quilt, I ran my hand over the backing. Yes, the muslin had been pieced together. A six-inch band ran across the top end of the backing. Then the rest was all one piece until I got to within ten inches of the bottom edge where the crackly part was. The seam was not as flat as the one at the top. Upon close examination the thread holding the two pieces of muslin appeared to be a lighter, fresher color.

Something had obviously been done here. It was not without great trepidation I got out my tiny embroidery scissors and snipped a few threads in the seam of my dear Aunt Sarah's quilt. Opening the seam about two inches, I poked my finger in and felt around. Yes, paper, definitely paper. I pulled the seam farther apart and reached in with two fingers. It was a large sheet of paper. Now I opened the whole seam. The entire end of the quilt was filled with papers each and every one of them elaborately decorated with all sorts of ornate scroll work. Some had pictures of ladies wearing Roman-like gowns. I pulled them out: 500 shares, 100 shares, 50 shares. All of them were stock certificates. In all, a couple thousand shares and all from large companies like Proctor and Gamble, GM, and so forth. A white envelope was among the stock certificates. My name was on it. I was so excited; maybe these were actually meant for me. My stomach whooped, and my throat went dry. Gingerly, I pulled a letter from the envelope. I wasn't sure I wanted to know what was on it. Then again, I wanted to know so very much. It was handwritten and from Aunt Sarah. It read:

"Dear Anna, I have written to Cookie and Matthias this quilt belongs to you and I have left you a little something. I have done it this way so you need not have the trouble of dividing my properties among you. You see I have put your name on them all. You must take them to a lawyer or stock broker and have them registered so you can either sell them or collect the dividends. I suggest the latter. You can take them to Mr. Jepson and he will help you, I'm sure. I will be with the Lord when you read this, but I will always be thinking of you. Much love to you, your Aunt Sarah."

Lordy was this real? What was I to think? I knew nothing about stocks. What did she mean "sell or collect the dividends"? When I thought of stocks, all that came to mind was Wall Street, big dark buildings with men in dark suits going in and out. Not my family's kind of folks at all.

I jumped up and paced the room. Grandfather bonged three o'clock. I stacked the certificates into a neat pile. What was I to do? I wondered how much all this paper was worth. Something or nothing? What to do? What to do? I kept repeating to myself. Then I saw Aunt Sarah's letter lying where I had dropped it on the couch. I picked it up; holding it made me feel better. Glancing at it, I realized she had told me exactly what to do: call Mr. Jepson. Why hadn't Cookie said anything about this quilt?

I fumbled around in my purse for my cell phone. Kept dropping it and losing it amongst all my pocket book junk. Giving up, I opted for old technology and went for the landline in the kitchen. I had to dial the old phone three times before I dialed it right, I was *so* nervous.

Mrs. Jepson's austere cultured voice answered, and I squeaked out I needed to talk Mr. Jepson about stocks. She began to tell me he was not a stockbroker. I must have sounded like a five-year-old babbling on about stocks, quilts, a note from Aunt Sarah. When Mrs. Jepson heard me say "Aunt Sarah," she repeated it aloud. It was then I heard a man's voice:

"That must be Anna. Let me talk to her."

In a few moments, he had me calmed down and an appointment to see him tomorrow morning at ten.

Tuesday dawned a bright cool crisp day. Leaves were falling in a gentle, multicolored rain. It was the kind of autumn day that defines the season and that we sometimes wish we had all year. I showered, fed Rollo who soon left for a major hunting trip, and read the paper while I watched the clock. I would give myself a good half hour to get from my house in New Bedford to Marion.

When I rang the Jepsons' bell, Mr. Jepson answered the door himself. He was still limping a little as he led me this time into his home office. I handed him the papers Aunt Sarah had left in the quilt for me. He shuffled through them and broke into a big grin, his entire face participating and his eyes sparkling. "Anna, my dear, you have won the jackpot."

Later, the Jepsons made it all seem like a fairy princess world. Indulging me with coffee and cookies they carefully explained how to handle my newfound wealth. Not knowing anything at all about investments, I was much surprised to learn I could have quarterly checks sent to my house or direct-deposited into my bank account. It would provide me with some regular income. Mr. Jepson was not sure how much, but he said it may be enough to squeeze by in a pinch. Squeezing by in a pinch right now seemed like a fortune in relief from stress. I left the Jepsons with a merry heart.

When I was happy, I liked to see the scenery when I drove, so I took the state road home, Route 6, not the highway. I found myself stuck behind a long line of cars waiting for the Fairhaven-New Bedford bridge to swing open to let a fishing boat and two scallopers get through. I hummed "What Shall We Do with a Drunken Sailor," the only boat-related song I knew, as I watched the scallopers heading out to sea. The bridge swung closed, opening the way for cars to cross. Next came the "Octopus". Luckily, the traffic light was green when I crossed this multi-lane intersection and no elderly folks in motorized wheelchairs were trying to get across. Fatal accidents had occurred more than once because apartment buildings for the elderly stood next to this maze of roads. I turned left and then right up Union Street. When I got to Rockdale Ave., on a whim I cut into Buttonwood Park. Pulling into a parking slot, I got out and strolled around, still humming under my breath, looking at the ducks on the pond and taking in the beauty of the park's splendid old trees for about half an hour. Then, almost reluctantly, I went back to my car and drove to a little strip mall in Dartmouth and had a bowl of kale soup and a roll in the little café there which was known for its fine soup. I lingered until almost one o'clock, and then sped over to Shay's where Joe would be getting out of work. I was not a minute too soon. He was ambling across the employees' parking lot. I had so much to tell him about my new circumstances I had forgotten I was to meet with him.

"I thought maybe you had forgotten," Joe rumbled. He had wanted to talk over the "lock-changing situation" as he called it since it touched on his former profession.

Leaning against the hood of my car, we chatted for some minutes, mainly me babbling on about my aunt's stock certificates, now my stock certificates. Then getting in our respective vehicles we headed for Aunt Sarah's house. Joe wanted to check the windows and doors and make recommendations.

As Joe ambled around Aunt Sarah's property, peering into windows, pawing the window frames, and trying the front and back doors, I stood in the driveway waiting for his opinions. Three issues of the *New Bedford Standard Times* lay in the driveway. Funny, I thought, I hadn't seen papers there before.

"Ma'am, is this a good time to talk to you?" came a high-pitched, timid voice. I turned and saw a rail-thin boy about twelve years old looking at me from across the street.

"Of course. How can I help you?"

"Well, ma'am, you haven't paid for the papers in about six weeks."

"I haven't? Oh, I see you think I live here. You are the paperboy?"

"Yes, ma'am. You always put the money in that box for me." The boy pointed to my aunt's decorative little birdhouse she had hung years ago next to her front door.

I could see his hand shaking. "Actually, it was my aunt's house and she died several weeks ago. I didn't think about the paper and I haven't seen any in the drive before today."

"I leave them in the driveway and after a day or so, they disappear, so I thought she was taking them in. I guess she was real sick, huh? That's why she was so grumpy."

"I'll pay you for the papers." I opened my pocketbook and found I did not have enough cash. I sat in the passenger seat of my car and began writing in my checkbook.

Meanwhile, Joe had finished his survey and came up to where we were standing. "Why'd you think Sari was grumpy, son? She was the nicest lady in the world," Joe asked the boy gently, but his low voice and rugged visage frightened the boy, and I could see him fighting back tears.

"Because she kicked my dog." He grabbed my check and ran into his house across the street, not hearing my protests that my aunt would never do that.

After he went indoors, a woman came and stood in the doorway, as if trying to decide whether she should come over and talk to us.

"I think I should speak with her," I said to Joe and crossed the street.

The woman, Jamie's mother, told me they had never actually met my aunt, having moved into the neighborhood only a few months before. Jamie took over the paper route from another boy and did the same things he had done. Their little dog was a yappy one, she admitted, but there was no reason for her to kick it. "Puddles" had run out of the house to greet Jamie several times, as Aunt Sarah's was the last house on Jamie's route. Then one day, this lady was coming out of Aunt Sarah's house when Jamie brought the paper. "Puddles" ran up to him and started barking at the old woman. She kicked him so hard he later died at the vet's."

"How awful! At least let me pay your vet bills."

She demurred, but I insisted, and ultimately, she brought out the bill. When I saw the date on the bill, I knew my aunt had already been dead a week.

Handing her the check and teary-eyed myself, I said, "Must have been someone looking after the house, another relative, perhaps. She'd been dead a week by then."

"Yeah, probably. She was carrying stuff."

"Joe, what a day this has been. First, I'm up over the moon with happiness about the stocks and now this horrible thing. Poor little dog."

"There's more here than the dog, Annie. We gotta think about this. When you are up to it. And we still gotta get the locksmith over here."

But I decided I needed some quiet time. Joe would come over tomorrow after work and we would talk things over.

Chapter Twelve

In the evening I folded my aunt's eviscerated quilt into quarters and laid it over the far end of the sofa. I was thinking maybe I'd take it to the sewing group at her church to see if someone would sew it back together better than I could. I was not good with a needle and probably didn't even have one or any thread in the house, certainly not the right color or thickness, if, that is, thread came in thicknesses.

I curled up on the opposite end of the sofa with a mug of cocoa. I wanted to think everything over. I wanted to see if I could come up with any new ideas of who might have killed my aunt. I was sure it couldn't have been Steve, although, somehow, he had involved himself in something to do with my aunt's will. Sipping the relaxing chocolaty drink, I let my thoughts drift over the events of the past month: my aunt's death, or rather her murder, Steve's gambling debts, and his resulting horrible treatment of me. The arson, I had to admit, looked bad for my husband. Had he really done that? Had he faked a will? Left it for me or someone to find and then burned down the building that held the real and only copy of Aunt Sarah's will? Would it have been necessary to destroy an earlier will? I didn't think so. Supposing he had killed or injured Mr. Jepson? Unthinkable! But if he had done these things, was he also capable of killing Aunt Sarah? To get things started, so to speak, toward getting her money? How would he have known she had any money? I didn't. Oh, it couldn't be! Not Steve. Not my husband! And yet, he had become very strange. Now he was behind bars for weeks until his trial.

And then there were Marta's strange concerns, Cookie's suspicious trips into and out of the area, and Letitia's pushy interest in the violets. Were these women suspects, murderers? Marta, I didn't know well at all. For all I knew, she could be as nutty as the proverbial fruitcake. Would Letitia really kill for violet hybrids? She often told my aunt she'd kill for such lovely plants.

Would she really? I doubted it. Hopefully, it was just an expression. However, the boot footprints were feminine in size and the hybrids were missing. Perhaps I should pay Letitia a visit. But I'd take Joe along with me just in case under all those fluffy lavender scarves and purple ruffles there beat the heart of a murderous old bird. She'd not dare to choke or suffocate Joe. Yes, Joe would take care of her. In my mind's eye, I saw him reach out with those massive paws of his and she, squawking and flapping feathery purple wings through the air, swatting at his head.

My head jerked up. Grandfather was striking eleven. I had nodded off. A little cold, wet circle of cocoa lay across my lap where the dregs of my drink had spilled. Rollo was standing on the couch sniffing it. "Guess I drifted off," I said to Rollo, stroking his back. "I'm so tired. I dreamt Letitia was a flying purple bird, Rollo. Silly of me to suspect those old ladies, and besides, the cops had interrogated them all quite thoroughly. Pereira certainly seems a competent man."

But Aunt Sarah's house had, indeed, been broken into, ransacked, the hybrid violets taken, the other plants had their labels deliberately misplaced, Uncle Matthias' picture ripped apart, the walls marked up, and even Aunt Sarah's silly black cat clock swiped from her kitchen wall. All of this well after her death. Why? What hateful crimes! And now we knew the neighbors had seen a woman coming out of the house. So *that* at least was not Steve's doing. Unless he had a partner. I wish I had asked the neighbors what the woman looked like. Marta, Cookie, Letitia? Someone must have really had it in for Sarah. But how could anyone? She was so sweet, so good. Or was she? Was there a side of her I didn't know about? Apparently, she was financially very savvy. Maybe someone in her investment club. I didn't know any of those people. Hadn't I seen something in her desk, some papers about an investment club? I couldn't be sure. Maybe they were just papers from her broker. I'd ask Joe about it tomorrow when I saw him. After all, he had lived with my aunt, albeit briefly, but maybe he knew something about her investing habits. He did seem to know she was clever with money. I resolved to pay Letitia a friendly visit soon and look into the matter of the investment club. I would ask Joe to come with me just in case. Having decided on the next direction my "investigation" would take, I felt settled in my mind.

Rollo had crawled onto my lap and was kneading my thighs and purring loudly. His contentment somehow reminded me of the good fortune I had in all this; my aunt's wonderful legacy. I was no longer completely without income of my own. I wanted to daydream and make plans, but I resisted. I must know first how much it really came to. I had chatted with Roberta, the secretary of Steve's English department in the afternoon when I got home. We had always been kind of chummy. She had giggled when I asked, with much hesitation, if Steve would still be getting his pay.

"He is on sabbatical, Annie, he can do whatever he wants with his free time. Write a book, play golf or… whatever. We'll see where things are next June when he is due back," Roberta assured me.

I felt I was okay for a while at least. I would sleep well tonight. I was about to go up and get into bed when, pushing his sharp back toes into my lap, Rollo suddenly sprang from my lap. The neighbor's dog had begun to bark. Rollo despised that mutt who had charged after him when they were both young. The poor canine was now confined by an invisible fence. But Rollo had chased the dog through his own yard and scratched his nose more than once. However, the old mutt was a good watchdog. I could tell by his bark something was up. I went to the front window. A big black car was slowly

Barbara E. Moss

passing before my house. It stopped. In the dark, for I had no porch light on and my shades were drawn, from behind the edge of the shade I saw a man run up to my front porch carrying something on thick rope and drop it on my doorstep. He turned and hurried to the car, got in, and it sped off.

My heart was in my throat. A chill ran down my back. I ran through the house making sure all doors and windows were locked and turning off any lights I didn't absolutely need to see by. There was no way I wanted to be alone. But I was. Maybe it was an innocent prank. Halloween was fast approaching. But I had a feeling it wasn't a Halloween trick. How I wished I could talk to Joe, but he had no phone. I waited an hour. I would not sleep now until I knew what was on my porch.

It was well after midnight when I unlocked the front door and put on the porch light. Cracking the door open, I peered out looking first left, then right, and then feeling a little reassured looked straight across my yard and to the road. I saw nothing unusual, so I pulled the door fully open. No one was about, no cars, no nothing. Then I looked down at my feet where the thing was dropped. On my porch was a large black cat, very dead, much flattened, with tire marks across his middle.

182

Around its neck, a wire was drawn tightly cutting into the animal's fur and extending several inches from its carcass. My stomach lurched. I pressed one hand against my belly as if to steady its swirling and the other hand hard against my mouth. Then I felt something swipe against my calf. I screamed into the night air and nearly jumped off the porch.

"Hiss! Meow!" Rollo, an angry Rollo, had followed me out the door. His back was arched and every hair on his body stood straight up. He spat, hissed, and yowled. Whatever he was saying, it was unprintable in English. He was sniffing over the cat corpse working from head to tail.

"Rollo, get back inside." I snatched at him, but his fur was silky soft, and he slipped out of my hands into the dark. "Rollo! Come back!" No use calling, but I hated having him out at night. His desertion, that's what I felt it was, made me feel very alone. And yet, he had a cat door and probably went out many a night when I didn't know it. I'd have to trust him, trust my cat. I rubbed at the bad spot in my back, thinking I'd rather trust him than many a person I knew.

Then, as I straightened, I saw it.

A white tag was fixed to the end of the wire. Even in the dim illumination of the porch light, I could see writing on the tag. "Rendle," I read. I squatted over the dead beast. It smelled; the sweet putrefying stench of death. Holding my breath, I twisted the wire to free the tag. I was about to upchuck my supper when the tag came loose. I dashed into the house, slamming and locking the front door and flicking off the outdoor light. For a moment, I stood with my back against the door panting as if I had run a mile. When I caught my breath and my heart had slowed almost to normal, I looked at the tag. On one side in heavy black ink was "Rendle", on the reverse some numbers and letters were scrawled: "This is you unless you pay up. G. R."

Again, a chill ran down my back. Then, as I stood staring at the white tag, I thought, *This is for Steve, not me. I am not responsible for his debts, and Steve is safe in jail.* But even then, I realized this amounted to a death threat. Even if he couldn't get at Steve, it should be reported. I would call the police in the morning and talk to Mr. Jepson at some point and Joe when he came to do the locks with me tomorrow.

Having decided how I would handle this ugly message, my anxiety melted away, replaced by exhaustion, and I yawned. My feet felt so heavy when I plodded up the stairs as Grandfather struck one. I fell into bed and within minutes was sleeping the sleep of the innocent, unaware as I was then, of the full meaning of the cat on my doorstep.

When I opened my eyes, the morning sun was blazing through my raised shades in a fury of white light. Last night I must have stripped and changed into my jammies in the dark and never drawn the shades, I was that exhausted. I rolled over and reached for the clock. It was ten. How could I have slept so long? But sleep was a good idea, so I stretched my legs and wiggled my feet almost down to the foot board and pulled the blankets smooth over my shoulders. Ah, to sleep. Then I remembered the cat. Not Rollo, but the squashed black thing on my doorstep. My empty stomach rolled. I sat up and thumped my feet to the cold wood floor searching with my toes for slippers. No slippers. I got out of my warm cocoon and began fetching clothes in earnest. No hanging around in my bathrobe today, I wanted to be on top of things, and that meant being dressed from the get-go.

Where was Rollo? Usually my Yankee work ethic cat was here to greet me, often with a mouse clenched in his jaws. I pulled on jeans, a shirt, sneakers, and a heavy sweater. Despite the bright sunlight, the thermometer in the window read just thirty-nine degrees.

In the kitchen, I started coffee and opened a can for Rollo who still had not appeared. I heard something outside. Was it Rollo? Not the squeak of a meow, but high-pitched human voices. Soft, young voices were whispering at my front door. *Ugh*, I thought, *I do not want to go anywhere near that door just yet.* Then the doorbell buzzed. I hoped it was kids pulling a prank, but the hushed voices continued, and the bell buzzed twice more. I guessed I'd better see what it was.

I eased the door open a crack leaving it on the chain. Two boys about ten or twelve years old dressed in fleece jackets and baseball caps on backwards stood there. They were sort of huddled together and one bit at his lip nervously. I recognized them as being from the neighborhood. Why weren't they in school?

"We're sorry, ma'am," one whispered as if he did not want to upset me, "uh, but is this your cat? I'm afraid he's—"

I cut him off with a grumpy, "No. It's not." Then, getting better control of myself upon seeing the shocked face of the child, I said, "Someone put that there last night as a mean joke and I haven't gotten around to disposing of it. I'll get some gloves and throw it in the trash. Thank you for your concern. You are good kids."

"Well, we knew you had a cat," said the taller of the two.

"Meow!" Rollo made his grand entrance.

"Oh, there you are! I was worried about where he had gone," I said, looking at the boys. I offered the boys hot cocoa, but they said it was an in-service day at school and they had to go to the store for their mom.

After they had gone on down the sidewalk, I went out and disposed of the dead feline using the same furry handle Ramona's thug had used. It was almost lunch time when I finished my breakfast.

By the time Joe arrived shortly after 1:30, both Pereira and Mr. Jepson had disabused me of my comforting notion Steve's debts were his alone to pay off. In fact, Pereira heavily suggested while they were indeed Steve's debts, considering who the creditor was, unless I wanted to become a widow, I'd better pay off his debts. He ended the phone call with the somber reminder that "accidents" happen in prison.

I had just set the phone down when I heard Joe's VW rattle to a halt out front. But a minute passed before I heard his door slam shut. I opened the front door and Joe was making his way up the front walk, his shoulders sagging and his arms swinging heavily at his sides.

I almost sang out, "What's with the King Kong walk?" when I caught the sadness in the burley fellow's eyes.

"Joe, what's the matter?"

"Nuthin'."

"Here, have some coffee."

I steered him toward the kitchen and set a mug of coffee on the table before him. He took one sip and set it down, sighed, and began playing with the mug; turning it one way and then the other. *Okay*, I said to myself, *if Joe won't talk, I will*, and I spilled out everything I had been thinking about, beginning with how I wanted to talk again with Letitia and wanted him to go with me.

In the cool light of day, it certainly didn't seem realistic fluffy Letitia would be dangerous and likely to attack me as in my dream the other afternoon. That was silly. I simply told Joe I thought she would be more likely to stay on topic if he were with me. Also, she might have the missing violets. Then, I launched into the part about the black cat and everything Pereira and Mr. Jepson had said.

When I had run dry, Joe said, "Yeah. You gotta pay the money." He got up and poured me coffee, took a swallow or two of his, and then said, "I came over to see you about the locksmith, remember? I got a good name for you." He wanted me to call the Alarms and Locks Security Company on Kempton Street, New Bedford. He pulled a crumpled slip of paper from his shirt pocket with the phone number on it.

I talked to a knowledgeable seeming woman at some length, with Joe occasionally feeding me information about what he thought I should want. We set an appointment for ten A.M. Friday.

"That's the soonest they can come," I said as I put down the phone. "Oh, I'm sorry. I forgot you'd be working then."

"Maybe I ain't."

"But, I thought…"

"It's my last day, Annie. I've been let go."

"But, Joe, what happened?

"Nuthin'."

He didn't want to talk about it. He slurped his mug of coffee dry and, pushing back his chair, got up to leave.

"See you on Friday."

Chapter Thirteen

I met Joe at Aunt Sarah's house shortly before ten. The locksmith arrived somewhat later and introduced himself as Jesse Parsons. He was quite short, only about 5'4", red-headed with smiling brown eyes. He liked to chat. He and his brother Jacob, he told us, owned the company. They were twins. "No one could tell us apart," he informed us. Except he was married, he said, chuckling, and holding up his left hand to show us the thick gold band. His brother was not.

Having completed what was probably his standard litany for new customers, he got down to business. After a few moments of conversation and a stroll around the inside of the house, we left him to his work. I'd return later and check on his work.

Just as I was about to jump into my car, I called out to Joe, "How about a cup of coffee and some lunch?"

He hesitated, glancing at his watch. "It's early yet."

"Well, by the time I get it made… You can read the paper."

"Okay."

Brilliant, I thought to myself. *Now maybe I'll find out more about his job loss and he can read the want ads.* Not that there were many these days. Of course, by the time I had driven the few blocks to my house, I was thinking I was a snoop and maybe a mother hen.

As I neared my house, I saw a black car parked out front and two huge men strolling up my front walk. Dressed as they were in filthy gray hoodies, black watch caps, and heavy work shoes, they surely were not Jehovah's Witnesses or Mormon missionaries. The black car reminded me of the dead cat "gift" I had struggled to push out of my mind while talking to the loquacious locksmith. These guys really looked tough and my heart was pounding. I was so glad Joe was right behind me. I pulled into my driveway and Joe rolled in, hit his brakes hard, and stopped a few feet behind me. That brawny man was out of his car and beside me before I had the car door closed.

"Let me do the talking, Annie," he whispered in my ear, grabbing my hand and giving it a squeeze.

Together we approached the visitors.

"You Rendle?" The giant stabbed a finger at me.

I gulped and nodded.

"We come for the money. Now."

"Who are you?" growled Joe.

"Who are *you*?"

"Cousin."

"Gerry wants what's his and now!" said the slightly smaller of the two.

The bigger of the two thugs slammed his fist into the palm of his right hand repeatedly, grinning and panting eagerly, as if suggesting what he might do to "Rendle" if she didn't pay.

"How much is it?" I squeaked.

Joe gave me a warning tug on my arm.

"It's her husband that owes. She probably doesn't know."

At that point the smaller tough, the apparent spokesman, felt inside his jacket and pulled out a wrinkled slip of paper and showed it to me.

"Oh my God!"

My knees folded beneath me and my yard seemed to swirl around me. I would have hit the ground if Joe hadn't grabbed me around the waist and hauled me up. He glanced at the paper and gave it back to Gerry's beef. With encouraging warmth in his voice, he totally surprised me saying, "We can do this, Annie. Gimme two weeks. By November 10th, I'll have the money for you." To the enforcers, he said, "Tell Gerry Joe Brown's word is good. The little lady, my cousin here, just has to convert some things to cash. My word." With that, Joe extended his big paw of a hand to shake with Gerry's enforcer." Somehow the gesture had its effect.

"Far be it from me to lay a hand on a lady," the brute smirked. Then he gave Joe a poke in the chest with his index finger. Joe didn't budge. "Humph," grunted the enforcer impressed perhaps with the old ex-con's strength. Then he snarled, "Gerry ain't gonna wait no more. November 10th."

As they walked away, the bigger guy, who had not yet said a word, said to his partner, "But Gerry wanted the dough today."

"Yeah, but it's her old man who owes. I ain't quick to punch up a dame."

"Might help."

"She don't come across we get her old man." He turned on his heel and shouted at me. "You hear that, lady? You don't pay, we get your old man. You tired of him maybe?" Giving me a knowing smirk and winking evilly at Joe, he got into their car.

As soon as the black car slunk a way from our house, I ran indoors and headed for the bathroom. When I emerged, shaky and swiping at my mouth, Joe had the coffeepot going and my teakettle boiling. Until then neither of us had said a word.

"65,000."

"Sit down, Annie." He pulled out a chair. "You still got that whale tooth, don't you?

"Yes, so?" It came out like a scared little squeak. Why ever was he talking about that old hunk of bone?

"After hearing about the dead pussy cat, I knew you was running out of time with Ramona. So, yesterday I made some phone calls from my landlady's. I made us an appointment at the whaling museum for this afternoon. They got these guys there who can tell you all about the tooth, and one is an appraiser who told me there is a big auction coming up in a few days. If we move fast enough, we can get that tooth in the auction. It may solve all your problems. I know it's a good tooth."

I still didn't believe the tooth was worth anything; certainly not as much as Joe was suggesting. So, trying to give myself time to think, I put some black bean enchiladas in the microwave for our lunch before I said anything. Then I slipped back into the bathroom and gulped down some pink stuff to settle my stomach good and properly so I could eat and get through this day. We ate.

"Joe. You go."

"Whassa matter?"

"I just can't, and I need to check on the locksmith."

That much was true. I should find out about the tooth, but somehow, I found it overwhelming. I didn't trust my insides not to reject my lunch and my knees, in fact all of me, still felt shaky.

"You might hafta sign papers and stuff."

"Say you're my lawyer."

Joe snorted and said rather hotly, "Get real. Do I look like a lawyer?"

I had to admit he looked more like one of Ramona's enforcers, at this point, unshaven as he was, than an attorney.

We stared each other down for a good minute.

"Okay," he said at last, "but you'd better write somethin' out for me."

Slowly, I pushed back from the table. Putting my hand against my stomach where the enchiladas were doing a slow paso doble, I understood at last why I did not want to take the tooth to the museum. It was connected in my mind to Gerry Ramona and his enforcers. How much more pleasant to think about the little red-headed locksmith securing dear Aunt Sarah's house.

I went out into the living room and fumbled through my coats and bags in the hall closet where I eventually got hold of the cold, hard hunk of whale ivory that was the scrimshawed tooth. I also retrieved my cell phone and, having no proper writing paper, pulled out a sheaf of paper from the printer in Steve's downstairs office. Back in the kitchen, I clunked the tooth and phone down in front of Joe, explaining I'd probably be home before he would be done, and I'd like him to call me right away and let me know how things turned out. Then we started composing an official– or at least credible—sounding letter, explaining the tooth belonged to me, but for reasons not mentioned I was entrusting Joe to have the tooth examined and valued and perhaps placed in an auction. This took us considerable time as neither of us were handy with words. It was getting close to the time for Joe to leave for the museum by the time we had the final wording. I typed and printed out our hopefully presentable document while Joe lumbered up to the second-floor bathroom to shave with one of Steve's spare razors.

Agreeing to stay in touch, with a call at five P.M., if not before, a smooth cheeked, respectable-looking Joe set off with my cell phone and whale tooth for the New Bedford Whaling Museum. Little did I know then I'd receive no five o'clock call.

I figured I'd meet with the locksmith mid-afternoon and, therefore, took my time cleaning up the lunch dishes, not to mention a quick swish of the half-bath toilet off the kitchen. Then I went upstairs to change into something cleaner and fix myself up little to look more civilized. But after one look in the mirror, I decided on a quick shower and a complete change of clothes. Confronting mobsters and bowing before the toilet bowl had left me sweaty and disheveled, to say the least. I settled on some beige wool slacks, white cotton turtleneck, and my old favorite forest green cardigan.

When I had headed up the stairs to make myself more presentable, a pale light flickered for a second in the hallway. It hadn't really registered with me then or I wouldn't have hopped into the shower. My mother had always warned against water, plumbing and electrical storms, as she called them. But when I pulled my suede jacket from the hall closet a soft rumble of thunder rolled in the distance followed by a spatter of rain. I shoved the jacket back into the closet and put on my old trench coat. Then I quickly trotted out to the car ducking raindrops. Loud thunder cracked overhead letting loose a pelting deluge of rain as soon as I settled into the driver's seat.

It was then I remembered I needed my checkbook to pay the locksmith. Too impatient to wait out the shower, I dashed for the house and slipped on wet flagstone, banging my knee. I found the checkbook in the kitchen drawer quickly enough, but when Rollo rubbed against my wet slacks sticking them against my legs, I saw I had torn a hole in the knee of one pant leg.

Okay, fool, I told myself, *what were you hurrying for? The man wants his money and he'll wait for me.* Lightning once again lit my way as I went up the stairs to change.

By the time I drove the few blocks to my aunt's house, the clouds had emptied themselves of their fury and only a few drops spluttered against my windshield.

Pulling up behind Jesse's van, I was much surprised to see both backdoors of the little truck standing wide open. Water dripped from the gear hanging on the inside of the doors. How strange he let his stuff get wet.

I got out of my car and went to look into his driver's side window. No one in the cab. I went back and checked the opened back. Jesse was not in the van. Hmm. He must be in the house. The rain was picking up again, so, hugging my shoulder bag close to my side, I hurried up the driveway to the backdoor. I saw there were footprints in the mud in Aunt Sarah's driveway, but did not pay attention to them. I should have.

The screen door was shut, but the backdoor stood open. The old lock was pulled out, leaving a round hole. Nothing replaced it. Thinking he must be inside working on the front door, or perhaps the windows, I stepped inside and nearly tripped over an open toolbox. Again, how strange!

"Hello!" I called out, but there was no answer. I ran down the center hall to the front of the house. Jesse was not in the front hallway, fumbling with a lock. Nothing had been done at the front door. I went through the entire house calling for Jesse, even opening the cellar door and shouting down the stairs. The man was nowhere to be found. Remembering I had his business card in my bag, I thought to call his office. Couldn't do that. Joe had my cell phone and my aunt's house phone had long ago been disconnected. Cookie had seen to that. There would be no unnecessary phone bills. What to do?

It was then I thought of my aunt's neighbor old Mrs. Tripp, who I had talked to before, asking her to watch for any intruders into my aunt's yard. At first, she said she was scared to do this, but had later quite taken to the idea of flicking her parlor curtain aside and spying on the comings and goings at her neighbor's house. She had supplied the police with some information that perhaps may yet prove valuable. I was quite certain if I had only noticed I would had seen her flick her curtain and peek out when I walked up the drive. Surely, she might know what Jesse was up to. At the very least, she'd probably let me make a phone call.

I could hear more rain drumming on my aunt's porch roof, really pounding down. Thunder banged close by, rattling the windows on my aunt's porch. Its ragged lightning scared me so much I turned and pressed my face against the kitchen wall. Again, lightning lit the sky. I counted the seconds until its thunder boomed. Three. Upon the next thunderous clap, I turned up my trench coat collar and, holding it tight around my neck, sprinted down Aunt Sarah's porch steps, across her driveway, and over the soggy grass of Mrs. Tripp's yard.

I had reached her bottom porch step when the old woman flung open her door. Her hair flew loose in wild yellowish white strands. Her eyes glinted brightly as lightning flashed and more thunder rumbled. Was she afraid of the storm? I sure didn't like it.

"Why, dearie, how nice to see you! Come right in!" cried the old lady, "where it is cozy."

I scooted into the her very warm and dry kitchen; just being out of the weather and in old Mrs. Tripp's snug room made me feel calmer. Taking a deep, relaxing breath, I was about to ask the old woman if I could use her phone, when I saw some sort of movement on the wall. Involuntarily glancing quickly to my left, I saw the pendulum swing of a black cat tail flicking back and forth on her kitchen wall. Turning, I took a good look. And, yes, there hung a silly smiling black cat clock like the one my aunt had so many years in her kitchen. It *was* my Aunt Sarah's clock. There was no doubt it was my aunt's clock. Aunt Sarah had splashed a little red paint inside the ears and made a green bowtie under its neck one Christmas when she had her whist group over for a Christmas party.

"That's Aunt Sarah's clock!" I shouted. "I'd know it anywhere. How did you get it?"

"She gave it to me, dearie," Mrs. Tripp attempted feebly.

"No, she didn't. It was still in the house after she died!" I yelled.

"Well, she always wanted me to have it. You don't know everything, dearie."

That was a possibility, I thought. After all, I had not known about my aunt's investments. I might as well ask her if I could make a phone call. "Mrs. Tripp, could I use your phone for a quick call? My aunt's house no longer has one, and I don't have my cell phone. I don't know what's become of—"

When Mrs. Tripp cut me off with, "Ho, ho, you want to call that big boyfriend of yours."

I thought the old woman was about to agree. Then, hearing a truck rumble down the street, I stepped over to her kitchen window. I thought it might be the locksmith coming back, perhaps bringing help for some problem, but it passed by without slowing. "I'm concerned about the locksmith," I said by way of explanation.

Then I saw them. From where I stood, out of the corner of my eye, I could see into the next room. Flowers. The colors were unmistakable. My aunt's violets. "You have Aunt Sarah's violets! She would not have given those to you. You stole them!" I screamed.

The old crone grabbed me by my shoulders and spun me around. Holding me close to her face, she spat, "That's the least I could do. The least I could take after what she took from me!" She was screaming now. "That bitch, that filthy bitch. I waited years for my chance."

"Chance for what? What did she steal? What did she ever do to you?" I was totally confused, angry, and frightened. "Look, you're hurting me. Let go of me!"

"You want to know? You want to know, do you? I'll hurt more than your shoulders and you will find your locksmith real soon." Pressing her hand around my throat, she shoved me against the wall. She squeezed until I became dizzy and the world grew dark. "No, I got better for one of her kind," Mrs. Tripp whispered, as if talking to herself.

She let out a piercing laugh, a howl. She pushed me to the floor and placed a foot across my hips. In an instant, she had pulled the belt from my trench coat and tied it tightly around my wrists, yanking until it cut into my flesh. I fought to get up, but holding me to the floor with her knee, she pulled off the tie from her apron. She had incredible strength in her fury. I struggled, twisting around and propping myself up on one elbow. She rammed me flat to the floor again and this time bound my ankles.

"You want to know what she stole?" In a rage, the old crone dashed into her parlor and came back with a much-yellowed picture. She shoved it up to my face. "Him! He was mine, and then she came home with him one day and he never ever looked at me again. That bitch! That whore!" It was Uncle Matthias's picture, him in a Navy uniform and looking very young.

"He'd never want you." That was all I could I choke out.

"I loved him. Always did. When he died, it was me who cried at the graveside, not old stony-faced Sarah, the bitch. Then one day some of her mail was left at my house. I brought it over to her, like the good neighbor I was. She asked me in for tea. And that's when she had her little accident. Heh, heh "

"My God! You killed her! You murderer! You witch!"

"You don't have your cell phone, do you? And no free hands to call, anyway."

I pulled my feet in towards my butt intending to push myself up against the wall, trying to sit or stand, but she shoved me down and, ripping off another piece of her apron, she shoved it into my mouth and gagged me.

"Concerned about that locksmith, are you?" She howled with laughter that subsided into a string of cackles. "You'll find him real soon, dearie, but it won't do either of you any good."

With that, she kicked me aside and opened the door to her cellar. Kicking me furiously and with much pushing and pulling, she maneuvered me to the doorway. Then, with one ferocious push, she sent me rolling down the steps.

The last thing I heard her say as I hit bottom was, "Enjoy your company, Jesse."

Chapter Fourteen

Black. Everything was black. How long had I lain there? Then I felt the pain screaming through me. A small square of light flashed by through the cellar window, and, for an instant, I saw something yellow lying near me and the letters L O C K on it. Then everything went black again with pain, horrific pain. I tried to move, but the pain made me cry out a muffled, almost silent, scream through my gag. I remembered no more until I heard a familiar low voice call my name.

"Annie."

"Joe?"

"Annie, you're in the hospital. You was hurt bad, but the doctors say you will be all right."

I opened my eyes and saw the outlines of a darkened hospital room and heard the beep, beep of some hospital machinery. I tried to turn my head toward Joe's voice, but it hurt so bad. I groaned. The room and Joe's voice drifted away. I closed my eyes and returned into darkness.

"Take it easy, Annie."

That was all I remembered.

Then came a time when sometimes I was aware it was daytime. Then again, everything was like a dream. I was thumped and bumped. That was all I could figure. Later, I understood the bed was being changed with me in it and various things done to my body. I didn't really know what was happening and didn't really care. Doctors and nurses came in and out, adjusting my bandages and various tubes. Joe kept returning. That was sort of how I counted the days, by his appearances.

Then my brother Bill started coming in the evenings after work. He probably had come before when everything was misty and confused, but I didn't remember it. As my head cleared, I realized Joe came in the daytime, but never in the evenings.

The days crawled by. Little by little, the two men filled me in as to what had happened. Then, late one weekend afternoon, they were both there. That's how I knew it was the weekend. My brother could be there the same time as Joe. Joe must have thought I was well enough to hear how things happened because he talked and talked.

It seemed Joe had returned from the museum visit eager to tell me how exciting the scrimshaw experts had said the tooth was. When he couldn't reach me on my house phone using the cell phone I'd lent him, he drove to my house. He waited at my house for me to return. When I didn't, he drove over to Aunt Sarah's and was shocked to find both my car and the locksmith's van parked with its backdoor still open. He discovered my aunt's house was open and no locks installed and went in to look for me. Not finding me or anything amiss, he then went next door to see if Mrs. Tripp had seen anything. The old woman, he said, was all sweet smiles, almost flirtatious.

Smiling, she held up an old house key saying, "Well, I guess I won't be needing this anymore. Maybe you could get that boy to give me a new spare. I couldn't."

"Something about way she talked gave me the creeps. She batted her scrawny, gray eyelashes like she was an ancient Scarlett O'Hara." Joe proceeded to imitate the effect of those rapidly beating eyes in his grizzled hound dog face, which made me laugh for the first time in weeks. "Not funny," muttered Joe and went on with his story. "'You didn't see nobody?' I asked her. And then she really laughed out loud. 'No bodies, no bodies!' the old bitch screamed." Joe stopped talking and stared off. "Gimme a second." As if it was too hard to say what happened next, he took deep breath and sat straighter.

"Go on."

When he spoke again, his words caught in his throat.

"What happened, Joe?"

"I saw your pocketbook lying on her kitchen floor. It made me really scared; made the hair stand up on my neck. I backed out of there real fast and ran back to my car. All the time she screamed from her doorstep 'No bodies! No bodies!' I called 911 from my car."

That was a long speech for Joe. He sat back and took a sip of hospital coffee from a paper cup. He began again. "I had some trouble 'splaining what I thought was happening, but finally the cops agreed to send a car. Annie, my old thieving instincts, I guess it was, told me to get out of the car while waitin' for the cops and look around. So, I took my flashlight and my picks, it was pretty dark by then, and started casing her house, stayin' well away from her, still saying stuff at the backdoor. I went lookin' around on the front and sides. The front door's locked. Then I see a cellar window and trained my light on it. I see somethin' yellow down there. It was the locksmith's yellow jacket. It moved slightly, so I knew he was in it. And figured you had to be there, too." He sipped more coffee. As Joe explained it to me, he went wild and started working his lock picks to open the old lady's front door. He had gotten it open and slipped in when the cops arrived. Mrs. Tripp was still standing on her back porch and howling with laughter. Hearing her, the police went to her backdoor as Joe came through to the kitchen.

"I yelled to the cops there was a man in the basement. At first, the coppers looked like they was confused, but then Mrs. Tripp started screaming and swatting at the cops, using talk I hadn't heard since I left the Big House. The coppers hustled the old lady out and followed me downstairs. You two was in bad shape. Scariest moment of my life. I thought you was both dead."

"Well, to make a long story short, she's now in the clink, and you two in the hospital," Joe said, ending his story. He finished off the coffee, wiped his hand across his mouth, then stood and pitched the paper cup into the wastebasket. "Night, Annie, Bill." Talked out, Joe shambled out of my room.

One evening several days later, Joe came in while I was sitting up with a dinner tray in front of me. I had cleaned up my plate of insipid hospital food pretty good and had a little coffee left in a Styrofoam cup. He was smiling.

"Hi there, bright eyes! Ready for some good news?" He told me I 'didn't have no money problems no more.'

I laughed and grinned ear-to-ear at the great news and Joe's wonderful triple negative. "That's great, Joe!" were my first words.

None of Gerry Ramona's men would be bothering me, he added for good measure. The debt was paid off with cash left over. The scrimshawed tooth and been auctioned off for $150,000. "I told you it was a good one," he crowed. He had put the remaining money in Mr. Jepson's keeping. "I figured you was trusting him." Then, before I could thank him adequately, he drained the dregs of my coffee and scooped up the packet of oyster crackers that came with my soup. "You never eat those," he said and got up and left.

A little later during the evening visiting hours, Bill came in shuffling, but with a determined look in his eye. He sat down and the first words out of his mouth were, "We gotta do something about Joe."

"Joe? What is it?"

"You know he lost his job."

"Yes."

"I got here early and met up with him as I was coming in. He's proud, but I got him to talk. He's given up his room at the rooming house because he is almost out of money. He is sleeping at a homeless shelter and eating once a day at a soup kitchen on Purchase Street."

"Oh, my God! Poor Joe. No wonder he snatched up my crackers and bread."

"Yeah, he's pretty down about it. Just shrugs and says, 'Well, that's what happens to ex-cons.'"

"There must be something we can do."

"Well, let's see, how do I put this?"

"Just say it."

"Steve's trial is not for another month, and assuming he's acquitted—"

"He won't be," I interrupted. "I have a feeling he's guilty as hell."

Bill sat still for a moment, stunned, I think, at my certainty, considering what he wanted to say. I could see he had something on his mind.

"Go on, Cracker Jack." That was my childhood nickname for Bill. He had been a bouncy little brother. Now he relaxed a little, slumping in his chair.

"Well, okay. You weren't thrilled when I told you I asked Letitia to look after the violets, so I want to be sure you're okay with anything I suggest."

"No, I wasn't, but it's okay now. She really is the best person to look after them, and I really hadn't thought much about the violets at all. Go on."

"You know, I've been trying to look after that cat of yours." My brother was not a pet person, especially not a cat lover. Rollo knew that and had never liked him.

"I get down there every other day or so and put out a big pan of food. I don't usually see him much."

"You don't go down *every* day?"

"Now, Annie, it's a bit of ride from Acushnet. And sometimes when I get home from work, with the kids and all…" Bill sat with his head hanging low.

I knew there was more coming and I wouldn't like it. After a long moment, I said, "Tell me."

"We-e-ll," he delayed, not meeting my eye, "it's just I haven't seen him for three to four days now."

"Bill!" I screamed and sat bolt upright, hurting in several places, but I didn't care. "You must find him!"

"Now, Annie, you mustn't upset yourself. It's just a cat."

"HE IS NOT AN 'IT'. HE IS NOT JUST A CAT! HE'S ROLLO. MY BEST FRIEND! LOOK FOR

HIM!" I was shouting so loud a buxom, plump nurse came running in, patted my forehead, and asked me if I wanted something to help me sleep.

I totally lost it; grabbing a tissue, I bawled. "I want my cat! I want to get out of here! I want to go home!"

"It's okay, dear," said the nurse soothing my arm and smoothing the bedsheets over my waist. "Doctor says you're doing really well. He thinks you can go home in two weeks if you have someone there with you." She looked pointedly at Bill. "Are you the hubby?"

"He's my brother."

"I'm her brother."

"Doctor Shearer will be here shortly to talk to you himself."

Bill stepped over to my sink and drew himself a cup of water. When he sat down again, he said, "I have an idea. You may not like it, but just listen a minute. Do you trust Joe? Aunt Sarah did. I checked with Mr. Jepson, He couldn't tell me much, said you should call him when you can, but yes, Joe came to him with the money."

"I trust him completely," I said thinking to myself Joe would never neglect Rollo.

Very hesitantly, Bill said, almost whispering, "Why don't you let him stay in your house for the next few weeks. He could bring in the mail, the paper, put lights on and off, making it look like you were living there. He'd see Rollo, if he turns up, is cared for."

"If he turns…" I reached for the tissue again as tears rushed down my cheeks reminded as I was of Rollo. I blew my nose. "Yes, ask Joe. Get Joe."

Dr. Shearer appeared in the doorway. "Are you alright?"

"Let me talk to the doctor, Bill. I'll see you tomorrow, maybe."

My brother reached over the bed and kissed me on my damp cheek. "Get some sleep, Annie. I'll talk to Joe."

"Thank you."

I thought it would be a hard sell. Joe was a proud man. Bill stopped at the shelter and found Joe that evening shortly before they locked the doors for the night.

Bill called me later. "He grabbed the opportunity saying he was awfully tired of sleeping at the shelter, not that they didn't manage it well, but the company didn't suit him.

Weeks later, Joe told me, with a little smile wrinkling the corner of his mouth, all those "low-lifers", recovering addicts and psychos, were not good company for any self-respecting ex-con. Apparently, looking out for Rollo was the clincher. I knew Joe had a soft spot for the big feline, but I didn't know how much he really liked animals.

The next afternoon they got me into a wheelchair and Joe and I went to visit Jesse who was on the floor above me. His brother Jacob was in the room with him and introduced himself. He looked exactly like the Jesse who had stood on the street holding up his hand showing his wedding ring. But Jesse's face was now scratched and bruised and his hands puffy, the swelling almost engulfed that ring on his finger. He had sustained a cervical fracture and was paralyzed from somewhere around his waist down to his toes. Jesse lay in bed with a great collar-like brace surrounding his neck and steel rods holding it in place around his head. No movement of the head or neck was possible. He rolled his eyes towards us to speak to us. There were tubes and cords attached to various parts of his body and beeping sounds and lights over his headboard.

Speaking in a weak rustle, he said he remembered me as the lady who wanted locks changed but wasn't sure where he had seen me. Joe, he did not know. And, yes, he was right he had never really met Joe, being unconscious when Joe and an EMT rescued him from Mr. Tripp's cellar. Then his brother spoke up. The man

Jesse had described as his quiet twin. He told us his brother did not get a great many visitors. He thought because his friends could not bear to look at him. He would be happy for conversation. Although I'd have to do most of it as Jesse was very weak yet. Jacob wanted to know the whole story about what had happened to his brother.

We began at the beginning. Leaving out the part about my aunt's talking quilt, I started with the violets and her murder. I even told him how Steve had been arrested for arson. I ended telling them how I went into my aunt's house looking for Jesse and thinking Mrs. Tripp could help, going over to Mrs. Tripp's. I toned down the part about all her crazy stuff, but with me being thrown down the stairs. Then Joe took over. Telling about the whale tooth, how he had had it valued, how he couldn't reach me, but eventually saw the yellow coat in the basement. How he used his lock picks to break into Mrs. Tripp's house and direct the police to the basement thus rescuing Jesse and myself.

Jesse perked up at this point. "Lock picks? You can use lock picks?"

Joe clammed up. But, for the beeping monitor over Jesse's bed, an uncomfortable silence filled the room. I felt an explanation was expected, but I wanted to put Joe in the best light possible. After all, he could have run off with the money from the sale of the tooth, he didn't have to confront Ramona's men and in so many ways had proved himself a dear and loyal friend.

"Er, Joe has quite a history. He was a trusted friend of my Aunt Sarah, and now he is my friend. He recently lost his job at Shay's and has not been able to find suitable work."

"Why'd you lose your job?" asked Jacob.

Joe shifted uncomfortably in his chair. Making up his mind what to say in his lowest rumbling voice, "I was in prison once. People don't like ex-cons." Even more softly said, "But, believe me, I ain't gonna do nothin' to get me sent back up."

"Tell me about it."

"No."

At that point, Jesse started to say something, but coughed. Jacob grabbed a water glass with a straw in it and offered it to his brother. Jesse was holding his call button and must have pressed it for a nurse came running in. After much fussing, pulse-taking, temperature-checking, she elevated the head of his bed, so he was sitting up a little and arranged pillows and bed covers.

"Jake, you're going to need help to keep the business going. Maybe he could learn the other side of locks," rasped the injured man. Was there a little spark of the old garrulous side of Jesse?"

"You mean, locking rather than unlocking?"

"Uh-huh."

Jacob looked Joe straight in the eye and Joe met his eye. Jacob started to say something about coming down to their office when two nurses and an orderly hustled into the room.

"I'm afraid I have to ask you all to leave the room for a few minutes. The ambulance is here. We have to get this chap ready for his big trip," said the nurse.

"They are taking Jesse to Boston," said Jacob.

I took Jesse's hand in my own and gave it a gentle squeeze. "Good luck and God bless," I whispered. "Joe, I have to get back to my room." I said goodbye to the two brothers and again wished Jesse all the best.

Joe wheeled me to my room. Retelling my story had tired me more than I realized, for I dropped off to deep sleep as soon as my head touched the pillow.

A few days later, when I next saw Joe, he was ebullient.

"I got a job! Well, they are gonna let me try see how I do."

"Joe that's wonderful. You'll do great I'm sure."

So, that was how Joe ended up with a job, an old car, and a house to live in.

At last came that wonderful day. I was going home! To my dear old house, my own bed, my own cat, my studio, and my kitchen. I looked forward to rattling around with my old pots and pans. Thinking about washing dishes, I could almost feel the coarse weave of the warm wet dishrag between my fingers and sinking my hands into hot, soapy, water seemed wonderful and soothing.

I still had to use two canes for steadiness for a while. Joe had been there ensconced in the house for a couple weeks, sleeping in Steve's downstairs study. Bill was not thrilled with the idea of an unrelated man living with me. But since I still had to use two canes for steadiness and for plain getting around, he agreed Joe should remain there for a while to see that I would be okay getting up and down the stairs and so forth. Of course. with Joe working now, he wouldn't be there most of the day, but he'd be there if I needed help getting going in the morning or upstairs again in the evening. I didn't expect I'd really need much help, but the company would be reassuring. Bill wouldn't worry so much about me falling, or whatever. Also, if Joe hadn't been available, they would have kept me another two weeks or maybe more. Or I would have had to hire someone to stay with me.

I came home on a Saturday. I guessed I'd always be a crier, but this time it was tears of joy that bubbled in the corners of my eyes as Bill pulled the car up to my house. Joe was standing on the porch as I struggled out of the car. For a fleeting moment, I guessed it was the desire to be mistress again of my own place. I hoped my volunteer tenant hadn't made a bachelor's mess of my house. Bill held the door open and took my arm. I fussed with getting the canes out of the backseat and positioned so I could walk. It was not so difficult. In fact, I laughed a little thinking what a scene I was making, traversing the short walkway with Bill at one elbow and Joe at the other. Then, oops, I got a sharp reminder I was still rehabbing. Going up the three porch steps was treacherous. It would have been easier, I think, if there had been a railing to hold on to, but when trying to negotiate the steps with the canes and my two "guardian angels" something black suddenly streaked by in front of me. One foot slipped off the middle step and I almost hit my nose on the porch floor. My "angels" hauled me up and I heard a loud meow. Rollo had come to greet me!

"Rollo, you was sound asleep on the couch," rumbled Joe. "He sure does love you."

I got inside and immediately plopped down at the kitchen table, hooking my canes on the table's edge. My eyes wandered to the coffeepot.

"Would you like some coffee?" asked Joe.

"Sure would. Here, I'll make it." I made to get up and knocked my canes to the floor with my knee.

"Take it easy, Sis."

"You ain't ready for the Olympics yet, Annie. Here, I got it all made." Joe pulled a couple mugs from the pile of sparkling clean dishes in the dish drainer. "Couldn't figure how to work the dishwasher, but there was only me here."

The coffee was delicious. It was a gourmet brand from Shay's. Special for my homecoming, Joe told me. I looked around everything in the kitchen was in place, everything neat, tidy, sparkling clean. I suspected he had even washed the curtains.

"As my mother would say, 'You sure do keep a clean kitchen, Joe.'"

Joe blushed and buried his nose in his coffee mug.

We three sat around the kitchen table and talked over cups of coffee; Bill checking out Joe and being, I thought, rather invasive of his privacy. He asked Joe where he had been sleeping in the house and when Joe told him in Steve's den because the spare bedroom was obviously my studio. Not too subtly, Bill got up, stretched, and said he had to use the "little boys' room." He went off to use the half bath on the first floor. I could tell by the familiar creaking of a door he was checking out Steve's adjacent den for signs of Joe living there before flushing the toilet.

"Okay," Bill said sitting back down heavily, "you and Steve are still married. Right?"

"Of course, we are. You know that."

My brother gave Joe a significant glance that was something more than a glance. Joe bristled and made to get up. "Listen here. I'm part of the deal to get Annie out of the hospital this week, remember? If you want to be here morning and night to help her up and down stairs and so forth, you can be. I got work and cash now, and I don't have to stay here no more."

"Sorry. Just being a big brother, I guess."

We were silent for a heavy minute or two as none of us knew what to say next.

Finally, Bill looked at his watch. "Four o'clock."

"Grandfather!"

The two men looked up at me as if I was crazy. "What?"

"The grandfather clock did not chime."

"Oh, yeah. It stopped. I didn't know how to wind it or where the key was."

"Look here. I had better be getting home. How about you order pizza and I'll pick it up and bring it before I go." Bill attempted to bridge the awkward silence, ask forgiveness and do penance.

"Great," I said.

And so, it was that pizza and beer was our first meal at home.

Chapter Fifteen

Joe and I settled into a comfortable routine. He would see me safely down to breakfast. After we ate, he helped me back upstairs and settled me into my studio securely behind my drawing table with my canes hung over the back of my chair. Only then did he leave for work at Jesse and Jacob's shop. I could not have had a more patient helper.

I loved my studio. I had furnished it in my favorite colors: ivory and a sunshiny yellow. I'd flung Aunt Sarah's quilt over a big chair. The room was small enough I could reach some sturdy piece of furniture, like my chair or my drawing table, if I had trouble with my canes and needed to grab onto something for balance. I had a hotplate and tea kettle handy, and Joe had supplied me with snacks, cookies, candies, chips, and various types of yummy junk foods. It was my happy place. The bathroom was between my bedroom and studio, so I could pretty much stay there all day if I wanted. I pretty much did. The mornings flew by as I worked on my postcards until lunchtime. Already, I had a new outlet for them: Bill had brought in samples to the hospital gift shop before I had been discharged. They liked the old New Bedford scenes and agreed to sell them.

Jesse was still in the Boston hospital where he would likely remain for some time. The locksmith business was struggling along. They really needed Joe to learn as much as possible as fast as possible. But Jacob, knowing my situation, was good about letting Joe come into work a little late and taking a longer lunchtime to get me fed.

The first couple days he brought me "delectable meals" wraps from Taco Bell, Whoppers, and Happy Meals. I could see myself piling on pounds soon and craved veggies. So, I put together a shopping list, and that first Thursday evening Joe loaded me into his VW and we went grocery shopping. I was embarrassed to use the humming and clicking wheelchair cart provided by Shay's, but it sure helped. Now, with a little advanced planning, I could quickly throw together some tasty, healthier lunches and he would not need to stop at Taco Bell's or whatever and take so much time away from work. Now he often brown bagged his own lunch. I still depended on Joe completely at suppertime to handle the pots especially the bigger ones. He loved spaghetti and we boiled up a lot of it. He didn't mind helping because he was getting home-cooked meals and we had agreed to split the grocery bill as soon as he got paid.

Steve had been in and out of the courtroom several times, but I had not seen him for weeks. He had been denied bail because of what I bitterly called his "flight into Egypt"; that dash he made to New Hampshire when the police told him not to leave town. I had put myself on Steve's visitor list when he was first incarcerated. Getting on the list was a complicated process involving a background check to see whether I had a criminal record and a whole lot of questions. Only very few people could visit any prisoner, and just on Saturdays.

Now that I was out of the hospital, bad as our marital situation was, I felt I was long overdue to see my husband, canes or no canes. So, on my first full Saturday home, I took my second trip out, escorted by Joe. It was to the old Ash Street Jail where Steve awaited his trial.

Joe saw me to the door but then returned to the car. He did not want to go through the extensive procedure. With his record and not being a relative, he probably would have been refused admittance anyway. I didn't blame him. He had seen enough of the bars and tiny peephole windows of penal institutions.

I braved the restless ugly crowd of mostly rough-seeming sorts alone. Word spread only the first twenty-five people would get inside. Wanting to be sure I got to see Steve, I became shamefully unladylike and rudely pushed and elbowed my way toward the gate, accidentally, on purpose, rapping several ankles with my canes and muttering, "Sorry, so sorry." By the time I got into the visitors' room, I had passed through two metal detectors, been patted down, had my canes inspected, and been divested of my purse.

It seemed an interminable wait. The other visitors, the occasional male, but mostly wives or girlfriends, some with small kids clambering around underfoot, pressed their faces against windows while speaking into telephone receivers to their loved ones. From the language I overheard, precious little love was evident. Then at last it was my turn. They brought in Steve. He was wearing orange scrubs and his feet and hands were shackled, leaving him enough chain to lift his telephone, with his left hand coming along with his right. We looked at each other through a small window with a crisscross grid of wire mesh embedded in it. We talked to each other using the telephones. Perhaps, worst of all, I could not touch him. No kisses hello or goodbye were possible, assuming I would want to kiss him, which I didn't, with the way things stood between us. But I felt a lump rise in my throat nevertheless and tears pushed against my eyes at the sight of my once beloved and arrogant husband reduced to a shambling felon, until he spoke.

Picking up the phone and leaning toward the grid as if it would make him hear me better, I said, "Hello, Steve. Are you alright?"

"Are you serious?"

"Well, I don't know what to say. You look thinner. Are you getting enough to eat?"

"You call that pig shit they give us food? I can hardly keep it down."

I didn't know what to say. I didn't know how much Steve knew of the capture of Mrs. Tripp and my hospitalization.

"I just got out of the hospital a week or so ago."

"Paradise compared to this hellhole."

I supposed it was in a way. I decided he would not be interested in hearing about my injuries or of the capture of Aunt Sarah's murderer. I sat for a minute, thinking. Still not knowing what to talk about, I tried to turn the talk back to him with: "Do you like your lawyer? Is he doing a good job for you?"

"That bird-brained a-hole. He is so dumb he can hardly walk across the frigging room."

"Well, then…" After a little more of the same sort of talk, I heard:

"**Time**." That came from the guard, a corrections officer I would not want correcting me. He was the size of two football players. He took Steve by his arm and practically lifted him from his stool.

I shouted into the phone. "I'll see you next Saturday."

"Yeah. Okay. Whatever." I think that was what he said as he dropped the receiver and turned away.

As I opened the car door and threw my canes into the backseat, I was batting back tears.

"How'd it go? asked Joe. Then he looked at me. "Not so good, huh?"

I pulled out a tissue and blotted the corners of my eyes. I was angry but wouldn't let Steve make me cry. I told Joe about my visit.

He was quiet until we pulled into my driveway when, in almost a whisper, he said, "He's not worth it, Annie."

"No! Please! I don't want to talk about him." I did really, but not then. I had had enough for one day.

"You gotta take care of yourself first, now."

Joe was right, and I knew it.

I continued to visit my husband most Saturdays with either Joe or Bill driving me to the jail. I followed his case through the court system. The weeks slowly rolled by. I listened to his ugly complaints, his mood swings, and his vile language directed at his lawyer, the prison, and mostly at me.

One day, I realized I had somewhere along the way stopped being so personally hurt by this angry, unhappy man in orange scrubs. This was not the Steve I had married. I would wait for him to be acquitted and then pick up the strands of our marriage and see where it brought us. I left my hurt at the prison gate and focused my energy toward getting better.

The weeks rolled by. Fall became winter. I worked hard at my therapy, ignoring everything else except my art. California could have had an earthquake and floated out to sea for all I knew. I rarely read the paper. I was usually too fatigued in the evening to bother much with the TV. After thirty-seven days, the therapist was coming to the house only once a week, and soon afterwards I did not need my canes full-time. Although I still often grabbed one, especially in the evening when I was tired, or for a little extra support on New Bedford's uneven sidewalks. Toward the end of January, my rehab people cleared me to drive—in good weather. Hallelujah! What wonderful freedom!

I took a second batch of my postcards to the hospital gift shop where they, true to their word, put them on sale. They paid me for them then and there and put the cards on a rack before I left the shop. What a wonderful feeling to leave the gift shop with some extra cash in my pocket!

The next day I took another batch to a local gift shop run by a friend of my late aunt. She put the cards on consignment but assured me they would sell fast, and I should check back in a week. She asked me if I could do watercolors. I said I could if I had to but didn't usually work in that difficult medium.

"It doesn't have to be difficult. Just a few simple swipes of color here and there over a Christmas scene and you could make very attractive Christmas cards, Annie. Or flowers for birthday cards. I'd be glad to sell them."

Flowers! Wow, what a great idea! I certainly knew what African violets looked like and could draw them easily. Although, I'd like to have real ones to look at when I drew them. A sort of artist's model. I drove home bubbling with ideas and excitement. I hadn't been so cheered in months. I chuckled to myself as I drove along, thinking of how Steve had always belittled my artistic interests and even my teaching. "Dumb kiddie play time" he once called my class, but now I was on the verge of true artistic success.

Once home, I tidied my studio. I got out my watercolors and made lists of needed supplies. Weeks ago, I had donated Aunt Sarah's violets to the African Violet Club to be distributed among its members; when I was in the hospital for so long and even when in the early stages of my rehab there was no way I could attend to them. Thinking back then I'd never be able to care for the delicate flowers, I even let the purple-robed Letitia have the hybrids, knowing that, despite my feelings toward her, she was best able to care for them. Now I would ask her, explaining my project, if I could have one or two plants back. I was sure she'd say yes. I called Letitia, but there was no answer and I left a message. Then, I thought of something else.

It was January and the time when hothouse orchids bloomed. I had once been to the huge orchid show on Cape Cod. What a wonder! I could not believe my eyes when I left the snow-covered parking lot and entered a world blazing with reds, purples, yellows, and every color in between. I'd have to find out when the show was exactly. It would be great to get some photographs of the beautiful plants and maybe even buy an orchid. I would make cards with orchids gracing their covers; Easter cards, Mother's Day cards. As I daydreamed about orchids, I wondered if I should get a decent camera. I was so excited. I couldn't wait for Joe to get home so I could talk to him about going to the Cape. I turned on Steve's computer and Googled the orchid show. I was too late. Drat! It was over. So much for that idea. Next year, maybe?

Then the phone rang. "Hello?"

"Dearie, how nice to hear your voice!" You could have heard Letitia, the 'Pooch', across the room. "How have you been?" she yapped.

I explained briefly about my hospitalization and my sales opportunity.

"Of course, sweetie, I'd be glad to bring you the plants. I have more than I have room for. Consider the hybrids yours. Eh, dearie, I have several appointments the next few days. We old ladies always do. How would next Saturday work for you?"

"Fine."

I hung up amazed at Letitia's graciousness. After a moment, I realized I had supplied her with a vast supply of new gossip. I'd given her a veritable scoop on info to pass on to her lady friends, none of whom I had seen or spoken to yet. It was easy then for her to be generous to me.

Saturday arrived a bright shining, crisp day. A little after ten the doorbell buzzed. On the porch stood Letitia and three other ladies all with tall cardboard boxes standing in front of them.

"Good morning, dearie. After hearing about your troubles, the ladies in the club insisted we take up a collection. A sort of 'get well' present. May we come in?"

"Of course. Oh, my goodness."

I stepped aside, pulling the door wide open, and they all stomped in, each lugging a box before them. Letitia glanced quickly around and settled on a bare section of living room wall across from Grandfather. Almost as one the women took out Exacto knives and began opening their boxes. It was then I saw they contained shelves, lights, and all the necessary parts of a three-shelf plant stand. I was speechless.

"Now, Annie, we'll have this together in a jiff. Why don't you put on some tea water?"

"Oh, Letitia. You did not need to do all this."

"Well, Sarah was a charter member of our club. We honor her through you. It was a unanimous vote."

I recognized Priscilla Bronstad as she got up from the floor where she had been screwing together the legs of the plant stand. She patted my arm quickly saying, "Sorry about what I said before." I think she meant her unfriendly comment at the church service. She slipped out the front door and was back in in two minutes with the assembly and use instructions.

I found my voice. "Thank you so much. I'll never forget this."

The plant stand was assembled, moved against the wall, the lights plugged in and tested. Then the women started bringing in violets. Two by two a parade of glorious blossoms marched into my living room and were settled on the new shelves.

"We weren't entirely sure which were your aunt's after all this time. Some may have been our own. We all have so many, but we did our best," said Priscilla.

Letitia now made a formal entrance as only she could with two of the hybrids followed by another lady with the other two. "Ta da! Look at the hybrids. They're beautiful." They were. Two were a deep royal blue with the tips of the petals softening to a powder blue. I hadn't seen them before. The other two bore the pale salmon and silver blossoms I had seen and watered in her greenhouse room. No wonder she thought of marketing them.

"Letitia, I didn't know she had blue hybrids."

"Those were in Mrs. Tripp's bedroom next to her bed. The police believe she took them earlier, perhaps the day she strangled your aunt."

"Oh, my God." I took a deep breath. "Well, I'm glad you all found them. They are exquisite."

Two of the ladies, whose names I learned were Joan and Betty, amused themselves skidding flowerpots left and right arranging the plants in pleasing color combinations. The hybrids were on the top shelf. Letitia and Priscilla meanwhile went out to their cars and came in with trays of sandwiches, cake, and pastries. Laughter filled the kitchen as we enjoyed and chattered over our delightful luncheon. Never once did they mention Steve, only relating stories about Aunt Sarah. Only when Betty noticed a few flakes of snow falling did the women get up from the table.

"Let me wash up these few things, dearie," Letitia offered, carrying teacups and spoons to the sink.

"No, no, no! You all have done so much. How can I ever thank you? Please get home while the driving is still safe."

"We meet the third Thursday of the month." Letitia gave me a quick hug and kiss as she slipped out the door.

I was sorting mail at my writing desk shortly after they all left, when I noticed a lavender sheet of paper had been slipped under the electric bill. It was an application to join the African Violet Club. It was filled out and marked "dues paid". *How kind of them*, I thought.

It began to snow in earnest and fat wet flakes slapped against my windows, then melted and ran down the panes. I spent the remainder of the afternoon making trial sketches of birthday cards. When I next looked out my window, the snow had turned to small cold flakes and the world was quickly turning icy white.

I went downstairs and made myself some hot instant cocoa to celebrate the snowfall and my happy new life as card artist and member of the African Violet Club. I had just sat down at the kitchen table and pulled up my chair when Rollo came bursting through the cat door. His back was sparkling with little snowflakes. The glitter on his black fur reminded me of a starry night sky. The big cat immediately trotted over to his empty dish, pawed it, and looking up at me meowed sourly.

"Okay, okay," I said.

I got up. Rollo circled my ankles, dampening my slacks with his starry snowflake sparkly fur. I grabbed a dish towel and tried without much success to mop him dry. Then I filled his dish with kitty crumbles and went back to my cocoa. I rewarded myself for cat mopping with two huge chocolate chip cookies. With so much going on in my life, I was not going to worry about putting on a few pounds.

The next couple hours I spent doing laundry, folding some clothes, and cleaning the bathroom, looking out at the snow from time to time, but thinking mostly about painting orchids and violets.

About three o'clock, I saw we had maybe two inches of snow that had turned wet and heavy again. I decided to sweep off the front porch. I got my broom and threw on my trench coat and made a stab at brushing off the porch. Nothing doing. This snow was too wet to sweep.

This was shovel work. I pulled on my boots and went out to the garage for the snow shovel. While probably not a good idea for a gal recently finished with rehab and one leg still noticeably weak, I nevertheless scraped and pushed snow around enough to make a strip down the center of the porch and down the walk to the sidewalk. Was I proud of myself for doing so much? I was outside maybe half an hour or forty-five minutes. The snow continued to fall, but at least I had made it less deep to walk through; it would be easier to finish the job later. Maybe Joe would do it or the weather would a turn warm and it would all melt the next day, as frequently happened.

Going back inside, I warmed up with some cocoa and settled down with a good book, wrapping Aunt Sarah's now-repaired quilt around me.

"Peace, be peaceful, Annie." It was Aunt Sarah's voice.

Was she speaking to me from wherever her spirit rested? No. It was my own thoughts. We had been so close if I thought of her, and the quilt always made me think of her, I could hear her voice speaking in my head. I felt very much at peace, sitting, reading, and sipping cocoa.

Five o'clock came and I thought about making dinner, five thirty, then six o'clock, I peeled potatoes and carrots, but no Joe. Whatever was the matter? He always popped through the door looking for his supper quite promptly. Was it the snow? I had a cell phone, but he still didn't. I set the table and got the coffee ground. I started pacing. I picked up the mail and looked through it a second time.

It wasn't until I was tossing out the junk catalogs I noticed the answering machine light was on. It was Joe. He must have called when I was out shoveling. He said he would not be home for supper. He had a call at the shop from some old buddies of his from Shay's and they were going out to eat and catch up, as he put it. Well, so okay, that was alright. I made myself a hamburger patty, boiled one potato and one carrot and sat down to my rather Spartan dinner. It felt lonely without Joe there. I had to admit I missed his rumbly, man of few words efforts at conversation. Besides his daily report of what went on in the locksmith shop and this evening, I had so much to tell him.

I watched TV until ten, went upstairs, showered, and got into my jammies and bathrobe. Sitting in a chair in my studio, I read, too curious about what Joe was doing to sleep.

At nearly eleven o'clock, I heard the front door open and Joe stomping snow off his shoes. I went flying down the stairs.

"That you, Joe? You okay?"

"Of course I'm okay." Joe's old hound dog face looked radiant.

I flew to him, grabbing his arms and was about to give him a big hug.

"Annie, I can't believe you waited up for me. I was just visiting some friends." He pushed me back a bit and planted a tap of a kiss on my forehead. "You don't have to be my mother."

I felt very embarrassed; could feel my face flush. "Yeah, I know. You're right." I pulled out of his arms and scurried up the stairs. "See you in the morning, then."

"Yeah. Uh, okay. Good night."

As I hurried up to my room, I realized maybe he had wanted talk, but I felt so embarrassed about acting like a mother, or worse yet, a wife. I wanted to get away.

I sat for a while. When I got into bed, I couldn't fall asleep. My mind was racing. What had I been thinking rushing into his arms like that? What was it with Joe and me? He'd been here almost two months now. Was he like a brother? No. Like a father? He was about fifteen or more years older than me. Again, no. Like a boyfriend or an old husband? An image popped into my mind of Joe's bulky body lying next to me in bed. Oh, dear, dear, oh, my! No! No!

I jumped out of bed, laughing. It was nonsense. I didn't want to think like that. I went into my studio and drew violets furiously until I was exhausted. About three A.M., I crawled back into bed.

The alarm was set, so I got up to get Joe's breakfast in time for him to go to work. I felt very awkward when he came to breakfast. Should I say anything about last night and my confused feelings? I decided I'd explain about the watercolor cards and show him the plant stand overflowing with violets. I could talk about that more easily. I need not have worried. For when Joe came into the kitchen. the first words out of his mouth after "Good morning," were: "Annie, you went off to bed so quickly I didn't have a chance to tell you my news."

I flicked on the coffeemaker, turned, and stared at him open mouthed. There was a sparkle in his eyes I had never seen before.

"News? You seem cheery. It looks like it is good news."

It seemed strange Joe having news. I did not think of him having much of a life. His activities and opportunities were often limited by his history. He wouldn't talk about his past even with me. I still did not know what had made him a criminal nor why he reformed and was adamant about going straight. I had to accept Aunt Sarah had trusted him and let it go at that. He had paid his debt to society. Yet, I had seen people turn their backs and walk away when they learned he had been in prison, and it distressed me to see him hurt. Jesse and Jacob were decidedly the exceptions. I could not imagine what his good news was.

"Last night, one of the guys from Shay's," Joe wasted no time getting into his story, "said he's getting married, see."

"Good for him. Will you go to the wedding?" I was sort of feeling my way, wondering if this could possibly Joe's good news.

"Maybe," said Joe distractedly, "but that's not the part I wanted to tell you. He is buying a house, see, and he's got this apartment that'll be empty, see."

I turned quickly away and pulled two coffee mugs from the cupboard above my head.

"Go on."

"It's small, just room enough for one guy, over a garage. He says it's nice. I'm going at noon to see it."

"Why?" asked dopey me. Then the dawn came. "Joe, are you thinking of moving out?"

"Yeah, sure."

I felt my stomach lurch.

He hesitated, then, in a rush of words: "It's kind of strange me living here. 'Specially now you don't need any help gettin' around. You being married and all. And I can go in and out without waking you up." He chuckled nervously.

I thought of last night. How I had run smack into him.

I was quiet. He was quiet. In a flash of understanding, and remembering Bill's reluctance, I had the realization he may have felt uncomfortable too. I poured our coffee.

Standing at the kitchen counter, I said, "You're right, of course. It is best. It's right. Of course, you're always welcome for Sunday dinner," I added, knowing how he had liked the roasts I always made on Sundays.

That was how our new normalcy began, me with my cards, and Joe with his new home and job.

That evening, when Joe came home to my house, that is, he was excited about the apartment. He wanted me to see it. We ate and then jumped into my car and drove over to Cottage Street to a charming old house two blocks north of Union Street. An addition had been built over a two-stall garage and this was where Joe's pal, the soon-to-be married Brian, had lived.

I pulled into the driveway, as per Joe's instructions, tucking the car in behind what I assumed was Brian's Corolla.

"The landlord says I can park my car on this side so it's off the street," said Joe.

There was a separate outside entrance up to the apartment. We started climbing. When we were halfway up the steps, the apartment door flung open and we were greeted by a tall young man with a mass of curly blond hair. His warm smile vanished when he saw me.

"I thought it was just you, Joe." His blue eyes gave me an appraising once over. His smile returned. I guessed he thought old Joe hadn't done badly for himself. "It is a rather small place for two."

"Oh, it is just me," said Joe.

I laughed and said, "I'm the soon-to-be former landlady, definitely not moving in. Guess he just wanted my opinion."

Just inside the door was a coat closet on the left hand and a tiny bathroom on the right. Brian wanted to show me the apartment, as if I had to give permission before Joe could rent. Brian opened the door to the bathroom and told me the shower had lots of hot water. There was no bathtub, but I didn't think Joe was the bubble bath type. There were two large rooms, a living room with a kitchenette along one wall and a bedroom. Brian had started packing up, so the rooms were in disarray. But Brian didn't want the kitchen appliances, nor the table and its chairs or the couch or bed. The rooms were bright and fairly clean. A little decorating would make them very cheery. But I hoped Joe would not want me to offer to do anything along that line.

"Anything I don't have to move helps me." The two men talked it over. Brian wanted the TV, but Joe got most of what he wanted.

I quietly sipped my coffee. After a while, I got up and started opening kitchen cabinets and drawers.

"What about this stuff?"

"Oh, I'll just throw that in with the rest."

"Whatdaya think?" Joe asked me.

"Perfect."

Joe wrote Brian a check and they went downstairs to talk to the landlord.

On the way home, I told him he got a good deal: a bed, a can opener, and a coffeepot. "What more do you need?" I said laughing.

Joe moved the next Saturday. The winter was mild, and spring was early. Joe still came almost every Sunday for his roast dinner.

It was one such Sunday evening I said, "You know, Joe, Steve's trial is starting tomorrow."

We had discussed Steve's trial so often that, now it was approaching, there was little to say. I'd watch it, of course. But I had made no decision on our marital future. Whenever I saw my husband, he was irritable and acted superior to the whole scene. He seemed to believe people like him, with his superior education and knowledge, should not be put to trial. For us, a lot would depend on whether he was acquitted. And even then, I knew I wasn't sure I wanted to stay with him.

By the end of the month, it was all over. He had been tried, convicted, and sentenced to seventeen years with a possibility of parole in six. The conviction took the starch out of Steve. I think he had really believed he'd get off. When I had last visited him, he was still cocky telling me how his now "very smart" lawyer would ensure the jurors chosen were not too swift. But when he was led away, my husband looked shrunken and dried up. His head was bowed. He gave me a longing look. Suddenly, I felt, despite everything and all our troubles that, at that moment, felt I still somehow loved and felt for him. I blew him kiss after kiss. He deserved that much from me. He was my husband still, and I would see him on Saturdays, but now it would be at the state facility in Shirley.

The courthouse steps were wet with melting ice. A damp wind blew. I shivered inside my heavy parka, but it was not the cold weather that chilled me. It was, I didn't know what; a strange empty feeling about my immediate future. So many *people* were gone: Steve, my aunt, and I saw a lot less of Joe. But *things* were actually okay. My art career had never been better. My finances, thanks to Aunt Sarah, dear Aunt Sarah, and Joe's help selling the whale tooth, were in good shape. But what would my life be like at this point? I shrugged my shoulders. Plenty of time to think, I guessed, when I got home.

I worked my way down the slippery steps and stood on the sidewalk waiting for Joe, who had watched the sentencing from the gallery, and was now bringing his VW around from wherever he had to park it, probably blocks away.

"How are you doing?"

"Oh. I don't know, kind of wiped out, I guess."

We drove home in almost total silence. When we got to my house, I said, "Joe, don't come in. I'll be alright. I just want to be alone for a while."

Joe pulled into the drive and leaned over and gave me a quick peck on the cheek. "You sure you're alright? Give me a call if I can do anything."

"I'll be fine. Thanks, Joe, you're a good pal."

I shut the front door quickly and leaned my back against it. The weeks and months of prison visits, the trial and sentencing were over. I let it all out, tears for all the pain.

Cried out, I went into the kitchen and sat at the table. Rollo came through the cat door, jumped up on the table, and sat next to me. He purred with a great ragged rumble. My good cat friend. Cats could be such a comfort.

The days rolled by. Yellow spring flowers were starting their conquest of New England's south coast. Sunshiny daffodils and forsythia graced just about every yard and roadside.

One morning, the doorbell buzzed insistently, I peeked through the sidelight and saw a tall man stood at the door. It was Detective Per Pereira. He was holding a large white plastic bag. I let him in.

"Good morning."

"Mrs. Rendle. Some unfinished business." The detective seemed uncertain as to what to say next. "Or rather, some finished business." He handed me the bag.

Inside was Steve's leather jacket. "I took the liberty of having it cleaned. No more horrible gasoline smells."

"Oh, good. Thank you. But I guess he won't be needing it for a while. Unless his appeal—"

He cut me off. "Haven't you heard from him or his lawyer?"

"No."

"His appeal failed. We won't be needing this as evidence anymore."

I mumbled something dopey like, "Oh. That's alright."

The detective seemed confused, raising both eyebrows.

"Well, you see, I have to get on with things, get my life straightened out. Been working a lot and don't look at the news much. But since you are here, what about Mrs. Tripp? I don't know about her either. When is or *was* her trial? No punishment would be sufficient for what she's done."

"There will not be a trial for Mrs. Tripp."

"What? But she killed my aunt, paralyzed a locksmith and put me in the hospital for weeks, and I still suffer from the injuries. Where is the justice?"

"Mrs. Rendle, Mrs. Tripp has been put in the Briarville Institution for psychiatric evaluation to determine if she is able to stand trial. Mrs. Tripp will be evaluated, and no doubt found to have a profound mental disturbance."

"You mean she is insane?"

"You could use that term. She will be confined and treated until she recovers. Your husband has a definite termination date for his prison term. Mrs. Tripp's release is determined only by the opinion of her doctors. I feel confident she will finish her days at Briarfield, in effect, a life sentence."

"I see," I said, satisfied Mrs. Tripp was being justly punished. "And, before you go, I have something of yours for you." I opened my writing desk and handed him a white square. "Your handkerchief."

"Why, thank you. I never expected to see it again."

"I took the liberty of cleaning it."

Pereira laughed.

I smiled and said, "Bye now."

The detective said, "So long," And, with a little shy smile, left.

I had a feeling I might see him again sometime, somewhere.

One Wednesday evening, the doorbell buzzed, and it was Joe. His old hound dog eyes were glistening with excitement. In his hand he held up a brochure. It was for a school with online courses.

"What's this? Private investigator?"

"Yeah, you can become a detective. I can study after work."

He was totally taken up with the idea of being a private investigator, pointing out, like his day job, as he was already calling his job with Jesse and Jacob, it put a legal use to some of his not-so-legal talents. He said he had the money for a computer and tuition, since he didn't spend much of his pay week to week. All he needed was a little help from me with the application. Joe's spelling and grammar were abominable. I agreed to do what I could for my friend who had done so much for me.

By the time I had managed to get Joe's application into acceptable condition, I was hooked on his investigator idea and applied myself. We were both accepted. We were now busy at our studies. I was already envisioning hanging out our shingle, perhaps bordered by my artwork and reading: Brown and Rendle Private Investigators.

The End